THE
BANGWELL BOYS

BEING THE SEQUEL TO

Hardiboy James; or, Chums and Chappies.

There v ere four of them, and they were making a horrible mess of it.

THE
BANGWELL BOYS,
A SCHOOL STORY.

CHAPTER I.

BANGWELL HOUSE—TWO UNFORTUNATE TENANTS —A FINE PROSPECT FOR THE BOYS.

OUR story opens about fifteen years ago, and the scene is laid in the town of Moatborough, famous for its age and many relics of bygone days.

It is not a cathedral town, as we daresay you know, nor is it a very busy town, nor remarkable for anything in particular except ancient buildings, churches, mansions, an abbey, and old age.

Of the latter, like some aged people, it is especially proud, and not without reason, for it is a ripe-old-Stilton sort of a place, with lots of blue mould damp and decay in its twisted, narrow streets.

At the time we write of it was a very sober town. The air of old age was upon everything, including its children, who played about the streets in a subdued manner, rarely breaking a window, never shouting or yelling, and if they fought among themselves they did it in a silent intense way that was especially their own, catching on and holding on until one had had enough of it.

The fight over, the victor would walk off with a suppressed smile, and the defeated one retire to some corner or lone archway to weep.

There was, at the time, very little life, and not an ounce of real fun in Moatborough.

Once a Punch and Judy visited the place, but only gave a single exhibit before it was warned off by the indignant inhabitants.

"They did not want their children taught how to break the peace," they told the exhibitor, and, without benediction, or gift of current coin, he went his weary way, invoking all sorts of things too numerous to mention on the heads of the people of Moatborough.

Suddenly a change came over the place, brought about by what was at first considered to be a foreign tribe known as the Bangwell Boys.

The manner of their arrival was as follows,

Outside the town was a long, disused mansion, as ugly as sin—outside, at least—and as commodious as an ordinary barracks. It was big enough to accommodate the retinue of a duke, but no duke wanted to live at Moatborough.

Nor would any of the inhabitants have it, though

offered at the lowest of rentals, because it was known to be haunted, and not even the Mayor of Moatborough, a thriving harness-maker, had furniture enough to fill it.

This inability to let the place nearly drove to madness the landlord, a miserly-disposed old gentleman, named James Wardle, but more generally known as Golden Jimmy.

At length a happy idea occurred to him, and he advertised it in the London papers, thus—

"COUNTRY MANSION to be let, *cheap.*— Suitable for a school. Commodious and convenient. Ample grounds.—Apply to James Wardle, Moatborough."

Two persons responded to this advertisement—

Mr. Josiah Bangwell and Miss Drucilla Fillwell, and the anxious Golden Jimmy hastened to secure one of them.

Now both the applicants, each ignorant of the other's application, found the place too big for them, and the accommodating landlord offered to let them half of it.

"By nailing up a few doors," he said, "and running up a wood fence down the grounds, back and front, it can be divided in two."

He offered the place at such a very low rental, and even in halves it would be sufficiently commodious, that both Mr. Bangwell and Miss Fillwell agreed to take half.

Nay more, led on by the artful James, they each, unknown to the other, signed a lease for seven years, one taking the north and the other the south end of the house.

And not until the business was done, and both had moved a lot of furniture in, and given up their old places, did they know exactly what they *had* done.

Then, for a brief space of time, the master of one school and the mistress of another were on the verge of frenzy.

They wrote to Golden Jimmy, asking to be let off, but he held them to their tenancy.

" I have done my part of the contract," he wrote; *" the intervening doors are nailed up, and I have erected a fence dividing the grounds into two, and you must do your part."*

Yes, he had put up a wood fence, about four feet

two inches high, and of the consistency of match-wood.

The boys and girls could talk over it, or walk through it, just as they pleased.

But Golden Jimmy had simply promised to put up a fence, and there it was.

If the tenants did not like it they were quite at liberty to put up another.

Now, as already hinted, Mr. Bangwell and Miss Fillwell were strangers, but misfortune brought them together and made them temporary friends.

They met and discussed the situation.

"If you manage to keep your boys well in hand," said Miss Fillwell, "nothing objectionable will arise."

"A little enforcing of maidenly reserve," said Mr. Bangwell, "will naturally lighten the difficulties of the situation." And here he became very impressive, "we must heighten the fence and strengthen it."

Then came the question about paying for it. Each thought the other ought to do it, as the landlord had declined to improve it in any way, but Mrs. Bangwell, a lady of a very decided turn of mind, came into the discussion and soon settled the matter.

"The boys won't mind a low fence if the girls won't," she said; "it is entirely a matter for you, Miss Fillwell."

The schoolmistress saw that for her own sake she must improve the fence, and with much bitterness she assented.

But the temporary friendship was at an end.

"If your boys are troublesome," she said, "I shall take legal steps to put an end to it."

"It is to be hoped that your girls will not be forward," said Mr. Bangwell, "for if they are I shall take means to publicly reprove them."

Then the meeting broke up, not in the most amiable fashion, and a fortnight later both establishments had fairly settled down.

The arrival of so many young strangers—there were thirty-seven boys in one school, and over forty girls in the other—aroused Moatborough from the apathy of centuries.

Some of the more energetic portion of the inhabitants took a walk at eve to stare through the iron gates at the boys at play.

First of all the onlookers were asked what they were staring at, and being either unable or unwilling to answer they were desired to "cut it."

Not "cutting it," according to orders, prompt measures were taken to drive them away. Tufts of grass, and peas forcibly projected through tin shooters, were among the most striking things employed to scatter the inhabitants of Moatborough, who, not being accustomed to warfare in any form, speedily retreated.

"We've got a lot of hornets come among us," said Old Mike Feeley, as he walked back to the town with several of his discomfited cronies.

Mike was the sexton and leading bell-ringer at St. Peter's church, the oldest and biggest in the town, and, among a certain body of antediluvian-looking men, he was an oracle, gifted with all sorts of intellectual blessings, among them the gift of prophecy.

"Mark my words!" he said. "We shall certainly rue the day Golden Jimmy let that old house of his."

CHAPTER II.

THE ST. PETER'S PEAL-O'-BELLS—MIKE'S WRATH AND VOW OF VENGEANCE.

IKE FEELEY lived up a blind alley dignified with the name of Crown-court. Who gave it that name nobody knew. As long as the oldest and toughest inhabitant could remember or recall by legend it had borne that name.

The old sexton lived alone, partly because he desired it, and partly because it would have been a tough job for him to find anybody to live with him.

Once upon a time, so long ago that it may be put down as ancient history, he had possessed a wife—a little, meek, silent woman, who was rarely seen abroad, and never except when the necessities of marketing brought her forth from home.

Home! What a home with a taciturn, bone-grubbing, ghoul-like, earthy old man.

Mike had always been old, so it was said, and for years and years prior to the opening of our story no change had been seen in him.

Apparently he had reached the maximum of man's age and stopped there.

Well! Mike was at home, and alone, engaged in the congenial pursuit of looking over a collection of odds and ends he had gathered together during his occupation as sexton.

From the graves he dug he had brought out several curious pieces of jewellery, mainly rings, which, by the desire of men and women long ago forgotten, had been buried with them.

He had also a few skulls of various sizes and a number of bones, part of the frames of the departed, and for many years he had laboured to get a skeleton together.

A nice skeleton standing in the corner of his room would, from his point of view, have been most excellent company.

But Mike had no knowledge of anatomy and was far too stingy to have the work done by those who did. An unwholesome, malevolent, bitter old man was Mike Feeley.

"Ding-dong! Ding-dong!"

Mike with a quick, startled movement, raised his head from his work, and turned his small, evil eyes towards the door.

"Ding-dong! Ding-dong!"

"It is the bells!" he cried, hoarsely. "But who's ringing 'em?"

Now, the bells of St. Peter's were the most musical in the town. They were the pride of the place, and Mike, who added to his other callings that of leading ringer, looked upon them and always spoke of them as his own property.

"That 'ere Sam Barlow's been on the drunk again" he said.

Sam Barlow was one of his ringers, the leading one after Mike, and had a duplicate key of the belfry tower. Mike rose up and took a heavy-knobbed stick from a corner.

" I've often vowed I'd do it," he muttered, "and I'll thrash him now. What an infernal jingle ! They're all drunk."

He had only to go out of Crown-court, and walk about twenty yards, before he came to the church, which stood in a quiet, narrow street.

The door of the belfry was in the north side of the tower, just within the churchyard.

Mike, who was very active for his years, hurried on, and entering the churchyared, saw that the door was open.

It was evening and the light streaming through the window showed four ringers at work.

Not men, but boys.

There were four of them, and with the exception of one, who was calmly ringing like an old hand, they were making a horrible mess of it.

One was being carried up by the swing of the bell wheel above, another was down on his back, with his foot in the slipper of the rope, and the third was standing with his back to the wall, holding on with a deadly grip to save himself from joining his companion aloft.

"Bangwell's little devils as I live !" hissed old Mike, and like a furious goblin, he rushed in to deal out destruction upon the invaders.

But he was instantly seen by the lad with his back to the wall, who shouted " Ware hawks !" in a loud, clear voice.

In an instant the boy aloft had let go, and came down upon the one rolling about upon his back, and the next instant both were upon their feet.

Old Mike aimed a blow at the boy who had been calmly ringing, which he dodged in a light and airy manner.

Then the whole four vanished like so many sprites out of the door, which they pulled to and locked.

A burst of laughter fell upon the ears of the furious Old Mike, who rained impotent blows upon the door, calling upon them to let him out on pain of future punishment of the most dire description.

But they only answered with a shout of derision, and a quick pattering of their feet told the sexton that they had left him a prisoner in his own belfry.

We pass over the next half hour—for this old man in a blind fury is not goodly company—and come to the time when Sam Barlow, a heavy, loutish kind of fellow, reeled up to the belfry door, and after sundry intoxicated efforts succeeded in opening it.

Unconscious of anyone being within, he was on entering struck down with a blow that would have battered in a less substantial skull than the one he possessed.

It did not even render him senseless, but, on the contrary, sobered him.

"You dog—you—you—" hissed Old Mike, utterly unable to find suitable epithets for him. "How dare you leave the belfry open to those boys ?"

Sam did not offer any explanation of his conduct ; but we may, for the benefit of the reader, offer it for him.

He came to the belfry half an hour previously with the intention of repairing the slipper of one of the ropes, and having got the key into the lock he thought he would just go and have "one drink."

The one drink led to two and three, as often happens in the case of topers. If it had not done

so in his case many of the events we are about to describe would never have arisen to be recorded.

He got up slowly, with his eyes on old Mike, and when upon his feet he stood still for awhile intently regarding him but uttering not a word.

The sexton returned his gaze with interest, his brows bent over his hollow eyes, looking as evil as ever man did in this world.

"You make mighty free with that stick o' yourn," said Sam, at last.

"I'll make freer with it," hissed Mike, "if you leave the belfry open again. Look at the ropes—half of em drawn over the wheels. Go up and put 'em right."

"Go up and do it yourself," said Sam, slowly.

"What, you won't ?"

"No."

"Then don't you set foot in the belfry again."

"I'll come and go as I like," said Sam, with a grin, "and *you* can't keep me out."

As he spoke he turned away, and with a heavy, slouching gait walked off.

Old Mike took a step forward as if to strike him again, but he thought better of it and drew back.

Muttering all sorts of anathemas on the heads of bell-ringers and daring boys he opened a cupboard, and took out a lantern, which had a small piece of common dip candle in it.

Having lighted this he closed the outer door, locking it on the inside to prevent further intrusion, finally walking to a low narrow opening in the corner.

This led to a winding staircase, just wide enough for a man to crawl up it. For two to pass each other was impossible, unless they were as thin and unsubstantial as many of the modern mashers. Above this staircase was the bell tower, which he gained, and proceeded to lower the ropes that had been drawn up too high by the swing of the wheels of the bells. And there for the present we leave him.

――――

CHAPTER III.

THE FOUR OFFENDERS—A PEEP AT BANGWELL SCHOOL.

WE will now follow the young gentlemen who as amateur bell - ringers had not, on the whole, made a very great hit.

In any other town but Moat-borough the jang-ling they made would have brought a mob of people to see what was the matter ; but the people of the old town were accustomed to occasional eccentricities of bell-ringing on practice nights when Sam Barlow had " had a drop."

Those who paid any heed at all to the unmusical sounds simply said that Sam was "worse than ever," and let the thing go.

The name of the youth who rang so calmly was Jack Wyburn, the leading spirit of Bangwell School.

A detailed description of his personal appearance is unneccessary, and we need say no more than that he was good-looking, high-spirited, and, in many ways clever.

The unhappy boy who had been drawn aloft was Bob Rudge, who was more often called Smudge, owing to his decided talent for getting himself into a mess.

If there was trouble about Bob was generally in it. If dirt was floating around Bob got his full share of it.

In school hours he embellished himself with ink in a ruggedly artistic fashion, and as for his clothes, they were spoiled as soon as they were put on new, and torn here and there with the least possible delay.

Harry Farnborough and Cecil Mead were the names of the other boys—very good fellows, fairly studious, moderately clever, and not averse especially in Harry's case, to a bit of fun at Bob's expense.

On getting clear of the churchyard, which they did with all speed, they sauntered on through the town, stopping to look at shop-windows occasionally and discussing their recent adventure.

"What an evil-looking old beast that sexton is," said Bob. "Why he looked *murderous*."

"He WAS murderous," said Jack Wyburn, quietly, "and if you had been there alone you would never have gone back to Bangwell School."

"I shouldn't have cared much about that," replied Bob. "Bangwell thinks a boy is made of leather."

"He'll make leather of you," said Harry Farnbrough, "if tanning will ever do it."

"I get licked for what others do," grumbled Bob.

"*Somebody* must get licked, you know," gently suggested Harry Farnborough.

Bob's answer was a shrug of the shoulders, which implied that he did not wish to discuss the subject, and then they sauntered on.

Presently they met half-a-dozen other boys, headed by a fresh-faced youngster who, with his cap very much on the back of his head and his hands in his pockets, looked the very personification of impudence.

This was Benjamin Chicks, an aspirant to the position of cock of the school, a position he had as yet not quite attained.

"Hallo! you fellows," he said, "what have you been doing?"

"Oh! just roaming about," replied Jack Wyburn.

"I say, Ben, you've one cheek rosier than the other. How's that?"

Both Ben's cheeks flushed but he did not seem disposed to answer.

One of the youngsters behind him supplied the information.

"He put his head in at the gate of the girls' school and the old girl was just inside. She boxed his ears."

"She didn't," said Ben, violently. "I knocked my head against the post drawing it back. So you just shut up, Davy Green."

"Anyway," said Davy, backing out of reach of Ben's arm, "the smack was like the crack of a whip, and I heard Miss Fillwell say—'There! that is for your impudence.'"

Ben walked on whistling, with an expression of irritation on his face, which mainly arose from his observing that Jack Wyatt was quietly laughing.

"Where are you are going to?" bawled Bob. "Can't you hear the bell ringing?"

This was the school bell summoning those who had short leave of absence to return.

There was a great deal of bell ringing done at Bangwell School. The boys were rung up in the morning, rung to meals, to school, to bed, and in and out to play.

The bell was a horrible nuisance to the neighbourhood, and the boys loathed the sound of it, for it was far from being musical.

There was a suspicion of a crack in it, and being rung by an impetuous serving man, named Biffins, it made a hideous row.

Ben did not favour Bob with an answer, but sauntered on, and the rest hastened back to school.

As they reached the gate, the sound of the bell ceased, and an usher came out of the house to check the boys as they came in.

He was a little, short, stout man, with a naturally comical face.

In manner he was very prompt, and his efforts to be stern partook somewhat of the ludicrous. In speaking he affected a deep tone.

His name was Roger Skaffer, and privately among the boys he was spoken of as "The Kaffir."

"Boys—fall in two and two," he thundered. "Forward!"

The boys, who had fallen into two rather serpentine lines, marched into the house two and two, the usher checking them off.

"Wyburn, Mead, Rudge, Farnborough, Green, Smith, Brown," and so on till the last had passed him.

"One short," he said. "Who is that? Wyburn—Mead—no, it's Chicks, the one boy to give trouble, of course."

He marched down to the gate and there ran against Chicks, who was just coming in quite leisurely.

"Chicks," said Mr. Skaffer, "did you not hear the bell?"

"Has it rung, sir?" inquired Chicks, slightly raising his eyebrows.

"Of course it has," said the usher; "but not half rung as usual. Go in to your evening studies and mind you get them up this time. You were very imperfect to-day."

The question, "Was I?" rose naturally to the lips of Chicks, but he checked himself and entered the house. Mr. Skaffer followed him into the hall, where a saturnine man in livery was winding up a clock.

"Biffins," said Mr. Skaffer, "you must ring the bell louder. Mr. Chicks, who has been in the town, could not hear it, and was late, of course."

Biffins wheeled round on the chair upon which he stood.

"Oh! he couldn't hear, couldn't he?" he said. "Didn't want to hear it, I reckon."

"Biffins," said Mr. Skaffer, severely, "you must not insinuate that a pupil of this academy is telling a falsehood."

"I don't insinuate anything," muttered Biffins, "all I says is that the bell couldn't be rung no louder if it was worked by steam machinery. I gets out of it all the sound it's got.'

Ben Chicks walked away grinning, and at the bottom of a long stone passage opened a heavy oaken door. The moment he did so the sound of many voices fell upon his ears.

It was the boys studying their lessons aloud, or in some cases, talking together "indifferent" as Mr. Skaffer would have said, "to the flight of the precious moments."

"Here, you fellows," cried Bob. "Biffins' got orders to put more power into that bell."

"Oh! lor," groaned several of his listeners. "What for?"

"Skaffer say's I couldn't hear it," said Ben, with a grin, "and that is what made me late."

"Something's got to be done to that bell," said Bob; "it isn't a fair thing to wake a boy with it. Every morning the clang of it gives me a regular scare."

The bell was indeed a perfect instrument of torture to those within and those without the house; but it was part of the place, and Mr. Bangwell was proud of it.

In addition to having it rung at the times we have specified, Biffins had orders to ring it every night at sunset. "Curfew" that was called.

Jack Wyburn said nothing about it aloud, but he and Harry Farnborough held a whispered consultation together, in which the word "bell" might have been detected by sharp ears.

Presently it was heard summoning the boys to bread and cheese and a mild form of non-intoxicating beer, generally spoken of by the boys as "wash."

This tempting supper was soon disposed of, and a hour later the boys were in bed.

A few words about the general establishment will not be amiss here.

First of all there was Mr. and Mrs. Bangwell, who had no children, but an adopted son, who was now about seventeen years of age.

The name he bore was Ned Goran, and he was a sort of pupil-assistant in the school. More about him by-and-bye. Then there were the two ushers—Roger Skaffer and Eugene Philpot—one we know and the other will reveal himself anon.

Last of all, there was a small staff of servants—three females, Biffins, and a boy who, inside the school, was called Cobb, and outside, by his intimates, Nutty.

The latter was a native of the town, and his valuable services had been secured shortly after the school was established there.

Of course his right name was known to the boys of the school, who, however did not confine themselves to it. He was known equally well as Chestnut, Filbert, Cocoanut, &c.

Now all these people were sound asleep at the hour of midnight, when a most alarming thing occurred.

The school-bell was suddenly rung with unprecedented violence.

Instantly everybody was awake.

Some of the boys tumbled out, and in the old sleepy style began to grope about for their clothes, until the voice of Mr. Bangwell was heard outside loudly asking who had rung the bell.

This question was supplemented by the silvery tones of his wife, who shrilly asked—

"Is it fire or thieves?"

Then ensued quite a babel of voices, in which the servants joined At last Biffins was heard by the listening boys to say—

"There's nobody in the ringing-room. They've cleared out, sir."

The ringing-room was not much bigger than a lumber cupboard, and on the ground-floor. It was left open to anybody, so that in case of any untoward event at night there would be no difficuly in getting at the rope-bell to give an alarm.

Immediately after this declaration of Biffins there was a movement outside, and the schoolmaster, accompanied by the ushers, began a round of the four dormitories in which the boys slept.

They were all out of bed, listening at the doors, and the scramble that ensued to get into bed again led to some confusion.

Some missed their bed altogether, others got into the wrong ones, so that in two cases at least, three of the boys were in one bed.

Mr. Bangwell was very wrathful at finding them awake, but the natural explanation that the ringing of the alarm-bell had awakened them he was obliged to accept as a sufficient excuse.

The object of the visit was to ascertain if any of the boys were absent—but they were all there.

"Whoever rang that bell," said Mr. Bangwell, "must have been very quick, for I was out upon the landing in an instant. Biffins, you sleep near the bell-room. Did you hear any sounds of feet?"

"No, sir," replied Biffins, who was in a very shaky state, and having in his fright put on most of his clothes the hind part before, was a pitiable object.

"Well, you ought to have heard them," said Mr. Bangwell. "Be pleased to—to—be—more watchful on another occasion. We may now all retire again."

There was a sound of movement, followed by a banging of doors, and then once more all was still.

The boys, being heavy for sleep, got into bed too tired to discuss the matter, and soon reached the l and of oblivion.

About half-past two everybody was awakened again, and by the same thing.

Loud rang the alarm-bell for a few seconds, and as before the scare was general.

Mr. Bangwell, the ushers, and the servants again, after a short delay to put on clothes, foregathered on the landing talking together.

Then came a ring at the outside bell which froze them into temporary silence, and an authoritative voice called upon them to open the door.

"Somebody go down and see what it is," said Mr. Bangwell. "Mr. Skaffer, please to see who knocks at the door at this unearthly hour."

CHAPTER IV.

A WARNING FROM THE AUTHORITIES—BENJAMIN CHICKS CAVES IN—THAT BELL AGAIN.

MR. SKAFFER and Mr. Philpot eventually went down together, the rest, consisting of the schoolmaster, his wife, and the servants, waiting, with palpitating hearts, for the result.

Biffins did not put in an appearance on the second occasion, and was, indeed, at that moment sleeping soundly.

"Who—o—o's there?" quavered Mr. Skaffer, stooping down so as to send his voice through the key-hole.

"Police! open the door," replied the authoritative voice. With much rattling of chains and jerking of bolts, owing to his trembling hands, the tutor complied with the request. Having opened the door, a sergeant and a private of police, each with his lantern turned on, strode into the hall.

"You rang the alarm-bell," said the sergeant.

"Why?"

"We—we don't know—who rang it," replied Mr. Skaffer.

Then Mr. Bangwell, finding that he could descend with safety, put in an appearance, and explanations ensued. The sergeant was very peremptory in his manner.

"False alarms of this sort," he said, "have to be paid for. It is a wonder you did not rouse the fire brigade."

"I am glad it was not disturbed," said Mr. Bangwell, wondering what use that brigade would be in case of a great fire. The sergeant was shown the "bell-chamber," and then the sleeping-place of Biffins—another cupboard hard by—was visited.

They found him lying on his back, snoring like half-a-score of grampuses.

It took a long time to waken him, and when his eyes were open he was so confused that he only half realised the situation.

He just made it clear to them that he knew nothing of the second ringing of the bell.

"If this sort of thing goes on," said the sergeant, fiercely, "the authorities will take steps to put an end to it."

He left with his man, who throughout had followed him like a shadow, saying nothing, and again the inmates of the house sought repose.

The boys went in for a third sleep, and, being unaccustomed to having their repose disturbed, slept so soundly that when in due time the morning-bell rang the majority of them did not hear it.

In Jack Wyburn's room not a soul awoke, and the consequence was that they did not put in an appearance at muster for morning drill.

It was under the superintendence of Mr. Philpot, who once upon a time had been a volunteer for a few months, and knew something about "fours," "right-about-face," the "goose-step," and other rudimentary military matters.

He was a very passionate man, and when excited was apt to be severe.

Finding the boys in Jack's dormitory had not appeared he flew into a rage, and with a cane—it was the popular instrument of torture in the school—hastened to quicken their movements.

On opening the door, and seeing them all in bed, his fury redoubled, and he went for the nearest sleeper.

This happened to be Bob Rudge, who had kicked off some of the upper clothing, and with only a sheet covering his body offered a tempting mark for the cane.

The first cut aroused him, and the yell he uttered awoke the rest, who tumbled out of bed, and catching sight of the tutor, began to pull on their clothes, wondering "What was now the matter?"

"The bell has rang half an hour," said the tutor. "Wyburn, you ought to know better than to encourage sloth."

"I am sorry, sir," said Jack, quietly; "but I don't think any of us heard it."

"You ought to have heard it," said Mr. Philpot, violently. "It's ridiculous—absurd to say you did not."

He raised his cane to strike Jack, who did not budge, but looked at him with a glitter in his eyes that showed his spirit was roused.

The tutor did not strike him but dropped the cane, and after another look round said—

"Be on the ground in ten minutes!" and left the room.

Poor Bob—who had been the only recipient of castigation—was still engaged in "rubbing out the smart" of the cut of the cane, making wry faces, and struggling manfully to keep back his tears.

"What a beast!" he exclaimed, "laying on to a fellow when he's asleep. I was just dreaming that I had a hamper from home, and was about to cut into a big cake, when—"

"He cut into you," said Harry Farnborough. "How lucky it is for some of us that you sleep in that bed."

"Oh! that's the way you look at it," growled Bob, as he began to wash.

Nothing more was heard about their being late at drill. If the tutor reported them, as he most probably did, Mr. Bangwell excused them on the ground of having been disturbed by the ringing of the bell in the night time.

Who did it? That was the mystery.

In accordance with an old custom the boys were asked one by one if they knew anything of the matter, *and one and all denied it.*

They passed through this ordeal at the close of the morning studies, and on being dismissed went out in a body to the playground.

"Somebody's being lying just now," said Benjamin Chicks, in a loud tone.

Jack Wyburn was just in front of him, and for some reason or other took the words to himself. Turning sharply round, and facing Ben with that curious glitter in his eyes, he said—

"What do you mean by that?"

"Why this," said Ben, coolly. "One of us rang that bell last night. I heard YOU talking to two or three about the bell, and what a nuisance it was."

"Then you suggest that I rang the bell?"

"You may have done it."

"And so told a lie?"

"Oh! don't you put yourself up for being better than the rest of us," said Ben, shirking the question. "Is it likely anybody would split on himself?"

"I ask you," returned Jack, speaking with the greatest deliberation, "if you mean to suggest that I have *lied?*"

"And I asked you," said Ben, turning away, "not to put yourself forward as a perfect saint."

"That won't do," replied Jack, laying hold of his collar and swinging him round. "Look here, Chicks, this is not the first time you have imputed objectionable things to me, and I won't have it."

Ben got through the first part of a smile, but the second half died away with an impudent answer that rose to his lips. He did not like the look of Jack's eyes.

"I *don't* impute it," he said.

"That will do," said Jack, and let him go.

Now there was nothing very alarming in this affair, but it practically settled a question which had for some time been in an undecided condition. It was, "Who shall be cock of the school?"

Jack's supremacy was marked from that hour, for the majority of the boys had stopped to look, and they perfectly understood that Ben Chicks had shirked an encounter with Jack Wyburn.

And Ben knew in his heart that he had laid down his chance of the championship. Bitterly he felt it.

His position will be readily understood by the majority of us, for we have all at times yielded in a moment of weakness to an opponent, and in most cases afterwards regretted it.

Ben felt as bitter in his heart as it is possible for a boy to feel in such a case ; but he concealed it. He had the power to conceal his motives and under a jaunty air hide his emotions.

His nature was revengeful, and there was a bit of the dog in the manger about him too. Ofttimes he would seek to prevent others enjoying that which he would make no use of himself.

"Jack won't be cock of *all* the school," he said to himself, "or if he is I'll make his crown an uneasy one to wear."

Schools are small communities, and are invariably split up into different parties. Ben could count upon a certain number of followers, who for their private ends would support him.

Despite Jack's denial it was freely whispered about that he had something to do with the ringing of the bell, and before night the rumour had somehow reached the ears of Mr. Bangwell.

It is not easy to say how such things are conveyed to the head authority, unless there is a sneak at the school, and such a thing was at present unknown in the place.

That night, or rather early the next morning, for it was about two o'clock, the bell was rung again, and the whole house was once more thrown into a state of alarm.

Mr. Bangwell turned out of bed, slipped on just as many clothes as were necessary, and ran into the dormitory where Jack slept.

He found him awake and out of the bed—and straightway accused him of being the disturber of the peace of the house.

CHAPTER V.

JACK UNDER A CLOUD—A DRAWN BATTLE—A LETTER FROM OVER THE FENCE.

VERY boy in the room was awake and heard the accusation, uttered in tones of unmistakable indignation. Jack's denial was instantly forthcoming.

"I am only this moment out of bed, sir," he said. "It was my intention to run down and see who it was that did ring the bell."

"Indeed!" said Mr. Bangwell, with an imperfectly concealed smile. "You must not tell that story to me."

"But I do tell it, sir," said Jack, firmly, "because it is the truth."

"We will talk of this to-morrow," said Mr. Bangwell, and stalked from the room.

Bearing a light in his hand he returned to the corridor, where he found the tutors with a scared look on their faces.

Each had a candle in his hand, which he held at an angle of forty-five, freely dropping the fat upon the linoleum-covered floor."

"Do hold your candles straight," said Mr. Bangwell, fiercely, "and come downstairs with me. Everybody else," he bawled, "get to bed at once."

The servant-maids, who were listening at the doors of their bedrooms above, obeyed him, and the three men went below.

There they found the door of the bell-chamber open and, as they expected, nobody there. But the rope was still quivering with the violence with which it had been pulled.

From there they went to Biffins' room and found him unmistakably asleep, snoring and gasping in the thick of some agonising dream.

"We need not disturb him," said Mr. Bangwell, "for of course he can tell us nothing. We have only to wait a minute to see if the police visit us again."

"Might I suggest a lock on the door?" said Mr. Philpot. "Biffins could keep the key in his room."

"I will do nothing," replied the schoolmaster, "until I find out for certain who the culprit is."

They waited for a little time ; but the police did not come, and they retired again to rest.

No further alarm took place that night.

The next day nothing was said about it, until after morning lessons, when Jack Wyburn received an intimation from Mr. Bangwell that instead of going into the playground he had to remain in the schoolroom. He also remained behind to have a few words with Jack.

"Wyburn," he said, as soon as they were alone, "if you will frankly confess that you are the author of this trick I will say no more about the matter."

"I have nothing to do with it," answered Jack, "and I know nothing whatever about it."

"Five hundred lines of Virgil," said Mr. Bangwell, abruptly. "I have good authority for saying that it is you who is at the head of it."

Then he left Jack to make the best he could of the punishment inflicted upon him.

Jack said nothing, but there was a fixed look on his face, as he set about his task. He did not rebel, knowing that the better course would be to get over it with the least possible delay.

He finished it, as he did most of his school tasks, rapidly, and was in time to join the other boys at dinner.

Although inclined to think that he had to thank Ben Chicks for the suspicions of the schoolmaster he could not quite make up his mind that he could be so mean.

He could be generous to a foe as well as a friend.

Cecil Mead sat next to him and supplied him, in a whisper, with the information that Mr. Bangwell had received notice from the police that he would be indicted for keeping a nuisance if his bell was rung at night again.

"Which makes him awfully savage," said Cecil, "because the bell is one of his pet things, you know."

"Somebody's playing the sneak," said Jack. "Have you any idea who it is?"

"Ned Goran goes a lot to his room lately," replied Cecil, "and he holds aloof from us."

THE
BANGWELL BOYS
BEING THE SEQUEL TO
Hardiboy James; or, Chums and Chappies.

"Don't do that, you cowardly beggar" Jack cried, pushing the ruffian back.

No. 14.

Price One Penny.

"Silence!" said Mr. Skaffer, who sat at one end of the table.

Ned Goran, it will be remembered, was a pupil teacher of the school, a waif and stray, in a sense, who had been left on Mr. Bangwell's hands.

He was a tall, dark, reserved, pale-faced youth, who seldom took part in any of the games or exercises of the school, and was not by any means a favourite

Jack cast a quick glance at him, seated at the table on the other side, and their eyes met. Ned Goran coloured and looked down.

"Hanged if I think Cecil is far out!" thought Jack.

At this moment Bob Rudge choked himself with a combination of meat, vegetables, and table-beer, and this act being put down to undue gormandising he was deprived of pudding for the day and banished from the room.

He went out, after favouring Harry Farnborough with a repressed smile.

The fact was, taking advantage of being his next door neighbour, Harry had applied a pin to that part of Bob's anatomy which in a pig is sometimes called the cushion, and this was the main cause of the choking.

Bob, with a wrathful face was waiting in the playground when the boys went out for half-an hour's relaxation before resuming their scholarly duties, and he immediately challenged the offender to fight.

"But you can't fight," said Harry, laughing.

"Anyway, I'll try," replied Bob, "I'm not going to be always made a butt of. Now then, do you want the coward's blow?"

"Don't be a fool," said Harry. "Why, I could eat you."

But Bob was not without pluck, and he insisted upon fighting. He was backed up by Ben Chicks and half-a-dozen others, who wanted to see the fun, and there was a general adjournment to a place in the grounds which was not commanded by any window in the house.

Jack was in no humour for a burlesque fight, and seeing Ned Goran sauntering by the gate, he resolved to ask him if he had taken to being a spy—a go-between the boys and their teachers.

"Goran," he said, as he came up beside him, "I want a word with you?"

"I don't want to speak to you," replied Goran, sullenly turning away.

"But you've *got* to speak to me," said Jack. "Is it true that you told Mr. Bangwell I rang the bell?"

"*What* is that?" cried Ned Goran, facing him quickly; "I go to *him* with tales. You ought to know I wouldn't do such a thing."

"But I don't know it," said Jack, "and I've heard you talk to him."

"It's a lie," replied Ned, abruptly, "and I don't want to talk to you."

Now Ned and Jack had never been friends, nor had they ever hitherto been enemies. The feeling between them had been that of indifferent acquaintances.

Therefore Jack was somewhat inclined to think that Goran, from his change of manner, was not telling the truth.

"Something's wrong between us. Goran," he said. "What is it?"

"Nothing," was the curt answer.

"There must be something?"

"Well, then, *I hate you!*"

Ned Goran fairly hissed out these words, and, swinging round, walked back into the house.

"I'm blessed!" was all Jack could say.

His meditations were cut short by a roar of laughter, and looking across the grounds he beheld the boys breaking up and dispersing.

Presently he saw Bob Rudge and Harry Farnborough assisting each other to dress, and sauntering up to them, he congratulated them on the amiable termination of the fight.

"Oh! it isn't all over," said Bob, "*it's a draw.*"

"How's that?" asked Jack.

"Why, it's this way," replied Harry, with twinkling eyes. "Bob can't hit me and I can't hit him, and we've been dodging about for a long time, and nothing came of it, so, as he says, it's a draw."

Jack saw exactly how it was. Bob could not hurt Harry, and Harry would not hurt him, so there was an end of fighting for the day.

The bell rang and the boys hurried in. Jack lingered until he was the absolute last and was about to follow when an envelope was tossed over the fence between the two school grounds.

That it came from one of the girls Jack readily guessed, and thinking that it had better not lie upon the ground, in case it fell into the hands of any of the "authorities," he picked it up.

Before he could see to whom it was addressed Ned Goran darted out of the house and seized him by the wrist.

"Give it to me," he said, hoarsely; "it's mine."

"What on earth ails you, Goran?" said Jack. "You go on like a mad fellow. If the letter is yours, take it. How on earth was I to know whose it was!"

He jerked his hand free, and tossing the crumpled letter upon the ground, walked into the house.

CHAPTER VI.

JACK AND BUCK GRUESUM—SAM BARLOW TO THE FORE—A BIT OF LOVE-MAKING.

IT was high noon—a quiet hour at Moatborough—when the greater part of the inhabitants were at dinner or asleep. In the High-street, the busiest part of the town when it was busy at all, only some half-score people were in sight.

Two of these were Jack Wyburn and Bob Rudge, who were out on leave for half an hour, Bob having received a remittance from home, part of which Mrs. Bangwell instructed him to invest in a few toilet necessaries, among them a tooth-brush and some powdered chalk.

They strolled leisurely down the street, passing Mike Feeley, who was on his way home. The old sexton, beyond a quick, malevolent glance from under his bushy eyebrows at Jack, took no notice of them.

THE BANGWELL BOYS.

11

Whatever else it lacked Moatborough did not suffer from a scarcity of beershops and public-houses.

In the High-street there was at least half a dozen of one sort and another.

Standing outside one of the least reputable of these, bearing the sign of The Gamecock, was a ragged boy about twelve years of age.

He was peering anxiously in at the door, evidently in search of somebody within. Who that somebody might be was speedily made manifest.

A ruffianly-looking fellow suddenly emerged, and before the ragged boy could get out of the way, smote him heavily on one side of the head with his clenched fist.

"Here again!" he cried. "Didn't I tell you I'd brain you if you come a-hanging arter me?"

The boy had fallen against a letter-box, half-dazed by the heavy blow he had received.

"Mother's got nothing to eat," replied the boy. "While you drink she starves."

The man, with a curse, stepped forward bent, as the action of his foot indicated, on kicking the boy.

Jack Wyburn stepped between them.

"Don't do that, you cowardly beggar!" he cried, pushing the ruffian back.

"Who are you?" growled the ruffian. "Get out of my way, or I'll kick you."

He looked as if he meant what he said, but Jack did not budge.

"Let the little fellow alone," he said. "You ought to be ashamed of yourself knocking your son about."

"He's no son o' mine," was the fierce reply; "but a brat as I took with a whining woman I married. Let me get at him."

Bob Rudge, who was a bit scared by the looks of the ruffian on Jack's account, called on the boy to get up and run away. Thus urged, he got upon his feet and staggered into the road.

Again the ruffian essayed to get at him, but Jack still pluckily stood between them.

"You shall not knock him about," he said; "he is no more than a child."

Growling out a fierce imprecation, the ruffian aimed a blow at Jack, who skilfully avoided it.

"Why don't you run?" cried Bob to the boy.

"I can't," was the answer he gasped out; "he's hurt me, and I'm giddy."

The ruffian was going for Jack again, being now half beside himself with rage, and would have done him some serious mischief but for the arrival of another party on the scene.

From out of the same public-house came Sam Barlow, just a "little on" with his great enemy—drink. He stared at the scene before him, and as the ruffian aimed a second blow at Jack he rushed between them.

"None o' that, Buck Gruesum!" he cried. "You are too fond o' hitting boys. Why don't you hit a man?"

The answer of the fellow called Buck Gruesum was a blow upon Sam Barlow's chest. He staggered back a pace and then went for the striker.

Science could not be expected, and neither possessed it. Three or four heavy blows were exchanged, and then Buck Gruesum went down from a tremendous smash between the eyes, which disfigured his face in a moment, as it were.

Neither Jack nor Bob had ever seen such a blow dealt before by the arm of man. It showed the tremendous strength possessed by Sam Barlow. It is doubtful if an ox could have withstood it.

The pale-faced, ragged boy covered his face with his hands and began to sob.

"Mother will suffer for this!" he cried. "Oh! don't hit him any more."

"I'm not going to do it," said Sam Barlow, "not until I hear of his beating your mother again. Hi! do you hear, Buck Gruesum?"

The ruffian was now recovering from the force of the blow, and struggling into a sitting position, he drew out a dirty red cotton handkerchief, with which he began to wipe his face.

"You boys get out of it," said Sam Barlow, "all of you. I'LL talk to him. Now, Dan Foster, off with you! I'll see that your mother isn't hurt over this."

The boy thanked him, and Jack helped him up the street, while Bob, who had a pretty good idea that something to eat would be acceptable to the poor lad, darted into a shop and bought a big loaf.

He was out again with it in a minute, and, running after the pair, thrust the bread into the boy's arms.

"There," he said, "take that home to your mother."

Dan's eyes flashed with joy, and just the faintest possible wolfish glare sprang into them. He was hungry, terribly hungry, and the impulse to tear away at that bread and devour the lot was very strong upon him.

But he resisted it.

"I'll take it to mother," he said, hoarsely; "she's almost starving. Oh! thank you."

The bare possession of food gave him new life and strength.

Forgetful of his weakness he ran off, and turning down a narrow sideway, disappeared.

"Bob, old fellow," said Jack, slapping his companion on the back, "if you live for a hundred years you will never do a kinder act than that."

"It wasn't much that I can see," replied Bob.

Jack gave him another approving pat, and together they proceeded to attend to their own business, which mainly consisted of the purchase of sundry toothsome things for a feast in the dormitory at bed-time.

Bob was, in his little way, a prodigal; money melted away from him like wax thrust into a fire.

A letter from home—a monthly affair—put him into possession of affluence for two days, and the rest of the time he was in poverty.

A happy-go-lucky fellow was Bob.

Boys are not good timekeepers, they are so apt to forget how it flies; and Jack and Bob lingered so long that they were late for dinner.

For this Mr. Bangwell thought fit to prohibit Jack's going out for a week. Bob was simply reprimanded.

"He seems inclined to be down upon you," said Cecil Mead, in the evening when it was generally known that Jack's out-of-school leave was stopped.

"He couldn't keep me inside this place for seven days unless I chose to stay," said Jack, quietly.

"Don't openly defy him," advised Cecil. "He can be very rough when he is put out."

"I don't care a straw for that," replied Jack. "If I want to go out I shall do so."

It was clear to everyone now that Mr. Bangwell had taken a dislike to Jack, and he made no concealment of it.

The ushers, of course, followed suit, and between the three he was for the next few days harassed in every way.

Every little error in his studies was made into a breach of discipline which demanded punishment. They burdened him with all sorts of things to be done out of school hours, and he quietly submitted, preparing the tasks allotted to him with the greatest facility.

But sometimes the curious gleam before referred to would appear, only to be dispelled by an effort of will.

"I'll go so far and no farther," he said to himself.

One evening—it was the third after the encounter with Buck Gruesum in the High-street—he was seated in the schoolroom after having got through with a "punishment paper," looking out dreamily, somewhat sick and sore at heart.

The rest of the boys were out for a walk with the ushers, "doing parade," as they called it, and the playground was empty.

Jack threw up the window, and, leaning back, fell into deep thought.

The situation for him was growing intolerable.

He could not account for the growing dislike of the master and ushers, which certainly could not be put down to the ringing of the bell, with which he was charged.

It had not been referred to again, and no further alarm had been created.

Some secret influence was at work against him. What was it?

While endeavouring to get at some solution of the affair he heard the front door softly open and close again. The door was on the left-hand side of the window, and beyond it was the high wooden fence dividing the schools.

The cautious tread of somebody over the gritty ground next fell upon his ears, and then somebody lightly tapped on the fence.

Jack was not troubled with idle curiosity, but he could not resist looking out to see who it was.

Kneeling down and with his eye fixed against a narrow crack in the woodwork was Ned Goran.

"That quiet mouse after the girls!" he muttered. "Who would have thought it?"

Ned's tapping was not responded to, so he repeated it a little louder than before. Then Jack heard one of the sweetest voices he had ever listened to softly reply—

"Why don't you leave me alone? I won't have anything to say to you."

"I can't help it," said Ned Goran, with a groan. "All I ask for is one kind word. I love you so."

"Nonsense!" was the answer, given good-humouredly enough; "you must not bother about me. I don't like you."

"You hate me, because I am a poor drudge," said Goran, angrily.

"I don't know who or what you are," said the girl, "except that you send me all sorts of letters, and I don't like it."

"Ah! I know who stands between us," said Ned Goran, with a groan. "It's—"

He dropped his voice, and Jack lost the rest of the sentence. Probably he would have caught it had he strained his ears in the true eavesdropping fashion, but he only took a lazy, amused interest in what was going on.

Not by any means was he prepared for the torrent of reproach that burst from the lips of the girl

"How dare you—you mean creature! I wish I had a brother — he would whip you. It's a shame!"

These and many other terms of reproach were heaped on Ned Goran, and finally he was commanded never to interfere with her again.

"In no way—no way," she said, "or I will get somebody to BEAT you."

Then Jack heard the pattering of her feet as she ran away from the fence, leaving Ned Goran muttering to himself.

Jack now remembered that Goran had feigned sickness at tea time, a headache, or something of that sort, and had obtained leave to absent himself from "parade."

The shamming was accounted for by what had just transpired.

Jack lying back in his seat again saw him walk slowly across the playground with his eyes beaming with a most unearthly light, and his cheeks as white as death.

Nobody seeing him at that moment would have accused him of shamming sickness.

At first it seemed as if he were going out of the gate, but suddenly wheeling he caught sight of Jack.

In a moment he stood like one transfixed, and then came hurrying up to the window hissing with the fire of anger burning within him.

CHAPTER VII.

COBB GOES A WOOING AND IS WOEFULLY TREATED —A MUSICAL SUGGESTION—JACK'S RESOLVE.

OU have been listening—playing the spy?" Ned Goran said.

"I have been sitting here," replied Jack, quietly, "and certainly saw some sort of tomfoolery going on."

"It is a plot for my humiliation," said Ned Goran, clutching the window-sill with both hands; "you are laughing at me now."

"Look here, Goran," said Jack, "I don't care a straw about your love affairs. You are making a bit of a fool of yourself. If it will be any comfort to you I'll give you my word that I won't breathe a syllable to anyone of what I have heard. In any case I don't mean to speak of it; but I'll be bound in honour to please you."

"Your word!" sneered Goran; "you who play tricks with the bell, and lie about it because you are *afraid* to speak the truth."

He was suddenly thrust back by Jack, who leaped out of the window, about as angry as Goran himself.

"You hound!" he said. "What do you mean by that?"

"I mean what I say," replied Goran. "Don't

strike me or I shall forget the difference between us, and *kill* you."

"The difference be hanged!" said Jack. "If you were ten years older, and as big as a house you should not call me a liar."

And then he rushed upon Goran, who closed with him, and a struggle ensued, which ended in a fall, Goran underneath.

"Now," said Jack, holding him down, "apologise for as good as calling me a liar?"

"I won't," hissed Goran. "Let me get up! I—I—"

"Here, what now?" broke in a shrill boyish voice. "Do my eyes deceive me, or is this a struggle unto the death, such as took place between the One Armed Avenger and the Ruffian of the Ribstone Rocks?"

These words recalled the combatants to themselves, for the speaker was none other than the boy in buttons of the house—Cobb, alias Nutty, &c.

Although born and bred in the town, he had from his birth risen above Moatborough, aspiring to make a name in the world.

Physically he was somewhat handicapped, for he was a veritable shrimp of a boy—undersized, with a small head, large ears, mouth to match, a pug nose, and eyes like two black beads.

"Well, well!" he said, as Jack got upon his feet, "it was a goodly fray. The victory's yourn, most noble knight. You got him down and held him."

"Get indoors, you impudent cur!" said Ned Goran, rising slowly, and brushing the dirt from his clothes with his hands.

"Steady," said Cobb. "Oh! ye adopted son of the house of Bangwell, I'm here on business. Evening post is in, I've called at the office, and there's a letter for Master Wyburn."

He unfastened the buttons of his jacket and drew out a common looking envelope, which he handed to Jack.

"There's the mis-sive, most noble sir," he said; "attached to a harrow and shot over the castle wall, as it might ha' been in the meadyevil days."

Jack took the letter and read the address, evidently written by somebody very illiterate.

"*marster wybun bangwell scole moatborrow.*"

The writing wobbled all over the envelope, and there were no capitals. Who could have sent him such a letter as that?"

Perceiving that the eyes of Ned Goran were fixed curiously on the letter, Jack put it into his pocket, and nimbly jumped through the open window back into the schoolroom.

"Right valiantly done, sir," said Cobb. "By my faith—"

But here he was cut short by Ned Goran, who dealt him a box on the ears that sent him staggering half-a-dozen feet away. Then the pupil-teacher strode into the house.

"'Tis well," said Cobb, striking an attitude, expressive of an avenging spirit within him; "a base, unmanly blow. But we shall meet again. Ha—ha! Villain, I follow thee."

Cobb did not follow Goran because the front door was forbidden to him, but he did the next best thing, by hurrying round to the servants' entrance, which would give him access to his foe—if he really desired to avenge the blow.

Jack, left alone, opened the envelope. Inside was a dirty strip of paper, on which was written—

"*buck grusum and old mike hev put their heds together—bewair.*"

. . . .

Situated as the two schools were, it was hardly possible for the boys and girls to long remain entire strangers to each other. Indeed, from the first there had been an inclination for them, as scientific men would say, to "gravitate" towards each other.

With only a wooden fence between the playgrounds it was absolutely impossible for two communities, inclined to hold speech with one another, to keep entirely apart.

Thus it happened that sundry holes of minute proportion had been made in that fence, through which a considerable amount of espying, and some whispering had been going on.

At first it was done without discovery, but the lynx-eyed Miss Fillwell soon discovered the work and communicated with Mr. Bangwell on the subject.

He, in reply, offered to punish the culprits who had bored these holes if Miss Fillwell would kindly point out who they were.

At the same time he ventured to suggest that possibly the girls were quite as bad as the boys, as she would possibly discover "if they were watched."

Now, as the reader is aware, both playgrounds were in front, but at the rear of each part of the house was a garden, separated from its neighbour, by a similar fence, and through the latter one solitary hole had been drilled, and remained there for some time unsuspected by either of the principals.

The culprit in this case was Cobb, who, seeing what had been done in front, and being a boy blessed with the imitative bump, had, for the purpose of communicating with one known as 'Melia Brown, whose occupation was connected with the seminary scullery, drilled an aperture through which they held some converse together.

'Melia was not a native of Moatborough; indeed, she was, as far as she knew, a native of nowhere, having been reared in the workhouse and taken therefrom when ripe for service by Miss Fillwell.

She, like Cobb, was endowed with a romantic nature, and so in due course they gravitated towards each other.

It was during school hours that they met, at what may be called the trysting perforation, and on the morning following the events narrated Cobb stole forth on loving mission bent.

He crept up to the orifice, put his eye to it, and saw nobody.

"Melia," he whispered, "are you there?"

Instead of hearing the sweet voice of his darling, he was staggered and astounded by the descent of a douche of cold water, pouring down from the top of the fence.

It fell from a bucket held by the fair hands of Miss Fillwell herself, who was standing upon a chair on the other side.

"There, you little wretch!" she said; "take that!"

"What—you doing of?" demanded the drenched Cobb.

"I've put a bucket of water over you," said Miss Fillwell, "and I'll drown you outright if ever you dare pry into my garden again."

"There's a law in the land," said Cobb, as he

scooped the water out of his eyes, "and I'll make you pay for this, Missis Spindles."

"You dare to call me names!" cried the irate lady.

"I'll call you what I like—Spindles—Shanks! I've *seen 'em* when you crossed the street on a muddy day—there!"

Miss Fillwell, exasperated beyond control, hurled the bucket at Cobb, and aimed so well that she knocked him clean over.

But the impetus of the act caused her to rebound from the fence and fall off the chair.

Cobb howled, Miss Fillwell shrieked, and, in half a dozen seconds, the servants of both houses were in the respective gardens.

Neither party could make much of what was the matter, and Miss Fillwell, recovering a little, got up and walked indoors.

Cobb, in no hurry to get over his agony, continued to roll about and howl.

"What's the matter with you?" asked Biffins, who, by the way, bore no love, either fatherly or brotherly, for Cobb.

Before Cobb could reply Mr. Bangwell appeared, and at once fell upon all assembled.

"What is the meaning of this disorderly scene?" he demanded.

"Cobb's got colic, sir," replied Biffins.

"I ain't," replied Cobb, sitting up. "I've been 'saulted and half drowned by Miss Spin—Fillwell, sir."

And then he proceeded to relate a story in which fact was blended with fiction in a masterly manner.

He had only just come into the garden to "tidy up the paths," when Miss Fillwell popped up over the fence, drenched him with water, and threw the bucket at him.

"And there's the bucket to prove it," said Cobb.

"But what had you done or said to Miss Fillwell?" asked Mr. Bangwell.

"Nothin', sir," replied Cobb, truthfully enough, "and I never spoke a word to her in my life, until she put the water over."

"Go in and dry yourself," said Mr. Bangwell, abruptly.

He took a very natural view of the case.

A very unjustifiable and unlady-like outrage had been committed upon an unoffending servant, and he would take steps to stop such proceedings in the future.

Accordingly he wrote a perfectly polite, but very sarcastic letter to Miss Fillwell.

He asked her if it was worthy of her to vent the bitterness she felt towards him, upon one of his servants.

"*A native of this town,*" he added, "*respectably connected and highly commended by the Vicar of St. Peter's.*"

Well, this affair made the breach between the schoolmaster and his neighbour too wide for a prospect of its being ever repaired.

But they communicated with each other no more for the present.

The story got about among the boys, and they enjoyed it exceedingly.

They suspected that Cobb was not quite so innocent as he pretended to be, and by skilful cross-examination got out of him that 'Melia was at the root of the matter.

Cobb vowed that he loved her true, and would never give her up for a hundred Miss Fillwells, and he was urged to do all sorts of things to get at and converse with his lady-love.

"If I were you, Cobb," said Harry Farnborough "I'd dress myself in my best next Sunday and call for her."

"She don't get no Sunday out," said Cobb gloomily.

"Write to her."

"She never had a letter in her life, and think Fillwell would be sure to open it."

Half-a-dozen of the boys had got Cobb to themselves in the hall.

Among them were Jack Wyburn, Cecil Mead, and Bob Rudge.

"I've a good idea for you, Nutty," said Jack.

"What is it?" asked Cobb.

"You sleep in the attic in front, don't you?"

"Yes."

"The window is in the roof and opens on the tiles. She is sure to sleep in one of the attics, too Why don't you serenade her?"

"That's a good idea," said Harry and Cecil together.

"But he'll want a banjo," said Bob.

"A banjo? You mean a guy-tar," said Cobb contemptuously; "just like the troubledors of Italy I'm on that job if I can get the guy-tar; it's in my line."

But there were difficulties in the way of getting guitar.

It is an instrument that costs money, and it very doubtful if ever such a thing had been seen in Moatborough.

"Failing a guitar, why not a concertina?" said Harry Farnborough. "I've an old one in my box It only wants a little mending about the bellows and paper and gum will do all that. Cobb, if you wish to have that concertina, it is yours."

Now, it so happened that Cobb for a long time past had been longing for a concertina.

He had indeed made several efforts to save money and buy one.

But, being given to reading tales of bravery and horror omnivorously, he had hitherto impoverished the bank and expended all his money in that direction.

He accepted Harry Farnborough's offer gratefully.

Jack joined in the general laugh when Cobb was gone, although he was far from being in a merry mood.

The anonymous letter he received a day or two before troubled him.

He had been warned against two men whom he instinctively knew could be very dangerous when roused, and he had undoubtedly excited the enmity of both.

But if they *had* put their heads together what would they attempt to do?

Jack did not exactly fear either, but the sensation of walking abroad with a powerful foe hovering around to do you an injury is never very agreeable.

"I don't like it at all," Jack said to himself.

After reflection, he gave Sam Barlow the credit of being the author of the anonymous letter; but he could not seek him in the day, owing to his leave being stopped.

Jack thereupon resolved to seek him at night, and run the risk of being discovered.

To go out after dark without leave was a daring thing to do, for if discovered the punishment would be very heavy.

But Jack was just in the state of mind to run any risk to gain a point he arrived at, and that night he resolved to go into the town alone.

CHAPTER VIII.

COBB SEES A DOUBLE GHOST, AND NOBODY WILL BELIEVE A SINGLE WORD OF IT—BOXED IN.

 OBB, among his other light reading, indulged in a great many ghost stories, which had the natural effect of giving him the jumps as he went about the old house after dark.

Biffins was a bit nervous, too, thanks to constitutional cowardice and when summoned to do anything about the place after sundown each laboured to put that duty on the other.

Mr. Bangwell's bell would ring, and then in the kitchen would come the wrangle.

"Cobb, it's your turn," Biffins would say.

"No it isn't," Cobb would reply, "it's yours."

Sometimes the cook would take the matter in hand, as she did on the evening following the day of the events just recorded.

Mr. Bangwell had a room upstairs, where he and Mrs. Bangwell often passed the evening. The bell rang, and Cobb, who had just finished reading a ghastly ghost story, nearly fell off his chair.

Biffins, who had been dozing off, woke up with a start. 'Neither offered to respond.

"Did you hear that bell?" cried the cook.

"It's Biffins' turn," pleaded Cobb.

Now Biffins and the cook had been chumming up of late, and as an inevitable consequence, Biffins had a supporter.

"*You* go at once," said the cook to Cobb, "or I'll—"

She looked round for the poker, and Cobb, knowing the lady's hasty disposition, got up and hurriedly departed.

He was filled with fear, soaked with ghastly records from head to heel, and he was ill prepared to meet the terrible shock he received.

On entering the hall he came upon two white figures walking to and fro.

Poor Cobb fell into a sitting position, and the two figures approaching him extended their arms over his head, uttering a monosyllabic but portentous warning—

"Beware—beware—beware!"

Then retreating backwards very slowly they reached the staircase, where they were out of sight, and skedaddled up to the next floor as fast as their ghostly legs could carry them.

Cobb sat for awhile in a state of semi-stupifaction; then, rising, he tottered back into the kitchen.

The look on his face, his trembling knees, told a story of terror that froze Biffins, the cook, and the two housemaids.

They all arose and Biffins made for him, catching the boy in his arms as he was about to fall.

"*Oh!*—OH!—OH!" he groaned.

"What is the matter?" gasped Biffins. "Don't tell me it's a ghost!"

"Two!" replied Cobb, with his teeth chattering like castanets.

After some time they got the story out of him, and a mortal terror fell upon them all.

Their first idea was to go to the "master," but the cook suggested the ushers, both of whom were in their special sitting-room above.

So they all went upstairs and knocked at the door.

"Come in!" said Mr. Philpot.

They went in and found the two ushers in a somewhat heated condition, sitting opposite each other with glaring eyes, and clenched hands.

Nothing much was the matter with them, but being opposed in politics they had got into an argument with the usual result, a row between them.

"Well?" said Mr. Philpot.

"What do you all want?" asked Mr. Skaffer.

"Cobb's seen a ghost!" replied Biffins.

"Oh! get out," cried both the ushers together.

They were not at all in the frame of mind to listen to a kitchen story of terror.

"But I assure you, gentlemen"—began Biffins.

"Get out!"

And out they went having nothing better in their minds to do.

The cook and housemaid at once glided downstairs, followed by Cobb, but Biffins, having through excitement lost two thirds of the strength of his legs could not keep up with them,

"Hi! stop," he groaned, "don't leave me alone to face 'em."

But they were gone, and Biffins had the whole of a long and rather dark corridor to travel by himself

Most schools suffer from a paucity of lamps and meagre fires and Bangwell school was no exception to the rule.

The hapless Biffins, thus deserted, was reduced to a state of limpness that rendered quick movement practically impossible.

He could only get along step by step, and he had not got very far when he heard a groan uttered.

It made him skip several inches in the air, and then he staggered against an old oak chest that stood against the wainscoting.

"Any port in a storm," sailors say, and nervous people when scared half out of their wits, will accept any place of refuge.

Biffins hastily raised the lid, and jumped into the chest, shutting himself in.

The next moment Bob Rudge and Harry Farnborough came out of a side room, and looked about them.

"What was that bang?" asked Bob, alluding to the noise made by the fall of the lid.

"I think it was this chest," replied Harry.

He raised the lid an inch or two, and catching sight of Biffins, hastily closed it down again.

"Oh! here's a lark," he said; "it's Biffins. Keep him in while I fetch some of the other fellows. Jump on the lid."

Bob did so, and Biffins, who now had got scent

of some of the boys being outside, tried to get out.

Bob put his back to the wall and pressed down the lid with all his might.

"You've got to keep there," he said, "till WE let you out."

Meanwhile, after the bell had rung again the cook had missed her Biffins, and, woman-like, reproached herself for leaving him in danger.

Mother-love is strong, and gives its possessor a marvellous courage when her offspring is in peril, so in a measure is the affection of a sweetheart, when a lover is a bit up a tree.

The cook called upon the others to go back to Biffins' aid; but they all refused, so she seized a short brush that was handy, and went boldly to help him, and, if needs be, save him from ghostly peril.

This time she did not go up by the main way staircase, but by a flight apportioned to the use of servants.

There was a door at the top which opened on the corridor, and as she turned the handle and peeped in she saw a sight which, as she afterwards said, "made her blood bile."

It was Biffins, half way out of the chest, struggling for freedom, while Bob, standing on the lid, was doing his level best to keep him a prisoner.

"You little villain!" she cried, as she went for Bob.

He saw his peril and attempted to jump down; but Biffins happened at the same moment to make a most strenuous effort to regain his freedom, so that Bob was shot into the air a foot or so, and then came down upon his back.

Before he could get up the cook was on the spot, and dealt him a crack on the head which made him see a jumbled mass of electric lights.

Bob kicked up and caught Biffins somewhere under the chin. The cook screamed, Bob shouted, and Biffins howled.

The row was prodigious, and a sound of opened doors and hurried noises now added to it. Bob, with some of his wits back again, scrambled to his feet and cleared out.

Then the two ushers and Mr. Bangwell appeared upon the scene, all in a state of excitement and thinking that, at least, ONE murder was being done.

Biffins was called upon to explain, and started off again with the ghost story.

He was once more angrily cut short, this time by Mr. Bangwell, and he, as the ushers had done before, refused to listen to a word of it.

"Go down to the kitchen," he said, "and stop there."

"But, sir," said Biffins. "Master—"

"I won't listen to a word of it," cried Mr. Bangwell, who had good reasons for his pupils' sakes for cutting ghost stories off at the root; "it is childish—ridiculous. Really, I feel ashamed of you."

So the cook, humbled and miserable, retired, and Bob Rudge, was by good luck, kept out of the business

But Biffins felt very sore over it, as he felt sure he would be the laughing-stock of the school, and he bore a bitter feeling from that hour against the hapless Bob.

For his present comfort he assailed the author of the ghost yarn, and cuffed him on both sides of the head as soon as he got near him.

Then, while Cobb expostulated, the cook fell upon him, too, and the housemaid also boxed his ears.

All round Cobb had anything but a joyous time of it.

Burning with his injuries he retired into a corner of the kitchen, and eased his feelings by reading his favourite penny horrible, " Left-Legged Jimmy; or, the Boy Terror of Blobb's Alley."

CHAPTER IX.

JACK IS MISSING—A DUMMY—WATCHERS OF THE NIGHT—A MISERABLE MORNING.

"ERE, I say," said Bob; "where's Jack?"

The boys had partaken of supper and afterwards been dismissed to bed. Jack was at the table with the rest and had left the room to retire with them, but now he was nowhere to be seen.

It was in the dormitory that Bob gave vent to this exclamation, and it drew the attention of the other boys to the fact that Jack was not with them.

"Oh! he'll be upstairs in a minute," said Cecil Mead, yawning.

"I don't think he will," replied Harry Farnborough.

"Why not?"

"Because I saw him take his cap from his peg in the hall, tuck it under his jacket, and make for the back door."

"Whew!" whistled Bob, "it looks as if he meant to go OUT."

Dead silence came upon them all for a few moments.

The idea of doing such an audacious thing as to go out at night—*without leave*—fairly took their breath away.

"You know Jack as well as I do," continued Harry, quietly removing his jacket. "He was forbidden to go out of the place for a week, unjustly, as he says, and that is the very thing to tempt him to do it. The week's nearly up, you know."

"What a mad thing to do," said Bob.

"I wish he hadn't done it," rejoined Cecil, "for if he's found out he will be dismissed from the school. Bangwell won't stand it."

"Oh! as for standing it," replied Harry Farnborough, "he'll do THAT, for he doesn't care to get rid of a pupil if he can help it; but he will make it hot for Jack."

"What are we to do?" asked Bob.

"Why, keep it dark," replied Cecil, "and when he comes back ask him not to do it again."

"Mr. Philpot goes round to-night," said Harry, "and he looks at all the beds."

"But he only just puts his head in at the door," said Cecil, "and a dummy will deceive him."

By general consent this was done.

The boys were very clannish in this dormitory and willing to run any risk and to bear stiffish punishment rather than betray each other.

The dummy they made was a fair representation of

They beheld their friend Jack lying upon the ground apparently dead.

a boy curled up under the bed-clothes and would suffice to deceive a person surveying the room from the door, by the light of an ordinary lamp.

In a few minutes all were in bed, lying still and waiting for results.

In due time Mr. Philpot came round and appeared at the door.

He had been renewing the political argument with Mr. Skaffer, and was thinking more of that than anything else.

As he appeared a close listener might have heard the "thump—thump" of the anxious boys' hearts as they screwed themselves up under the bed-clothes.

The usher only just glanced round and retired.

The dummy had served its purpose.

"He's gone," said Bob, in a thrilling whisper.

"Hush, you little beggar!" muttered Tom Drake, one of the quiet boys in the room; "if he hears us talking he will come back again."

"Then don't you talk," growled Bob.

But Tom Drake was so evidently in the right, that Bob said no more and the rest kept quiet for a while.

At length the whole house appeared to be still.

Sleep was for the time driven away from that dormitory.

Not one there could close his eyes, and the only relief to the monotony of silence lay in an occasional whisper.

There were several town clocks, the striking of which could be heard at night when the wind blew the right way. That night it was favourable.

First a little sharp striking clock announced the hour of ten.

CHAPTER X.

SPECULATIONS ABOUT JACK—BOB RUDGE GOES A-COURTING WITH FEARFUL RESULTS.

I N a few moments a deeper-toned clock announced the time. After that two or three more sounded the hour, and last and most correct of all, the deep-toned bell of St. Peter's Church boomed out.

"Ten, and not in !" said Cecil Mead. "What is he doing?"

"It is a piece of sheer defiance!" said Harry Farnborough, "he hinted to me that he meant to do it."

"He won't be able to get in now," said Bob, sitting up in the bed. "I can hear Biffins barring up, below. Oh! my eye, won't there be a rumpus in the morning."

"You may make up your mind to be in it," said Harry Farnborough.

"It's even betting on that," remarked Cecil Mead.

"No it isn't," said Bob. "I'm bound to get licked if nobody else does."

Harry got out of bed, walked to the window and looked out. A full moon was in the sky and below lay the playground, cold and deserted.

Beyond it he could see the housetops and church

spires of the town, but no signs of Jack or living thing.

"It's the maddest trick I ever heard of," he muttered, "but it is just like Jack. If he says he will do a thing he does it ; you can't stop him."

"But did he say he'd do anything particular ?" asked Cecil Mead.

"I am not going to say anything about it," replied Harry, moodily.

He got into bed again, and the boys lay still, silent and miserable.

Nothing more was said, but at last the deep breathing of one proclaimed that sleep had come upon him. It was infectious and one by one they dropped off.

About an hour afterwards Harry Farnborough awoke with a start, and sat up in his bed listening.

The movement he made disturbed his right hand neighbour, Cecil Mead, who asked if anything was the matter.

"I thought I heard Jack call me by name," Harry replied.

"Oh ! I had forgotten about him," groaned Cecil ; "perhaps he's below and can't get in."

"Suppose you get out of bed and see," suggested Harry.

A strange timidity was in the hearts of both the boys, who as a rule did not lack ordinary courage. Each hesitated to get out alone.

"YOU get out," suggested Cecil.

"Perhaps he will call me again."

They remained awhile quite still, and the only sound they heard was the footsteps of a night policeman, first faint, then stronger, then clearly, and finally dying away again as the man went on his rounds.

"I say," said Harry, "we ought to get out and see."

"All right," replied Cecil.

They got out together, and went to the window. The moon was now behind the house, casting the deep shadow of the building across the playground.

They could see nobody.

Harry opened the window and softly called to Jack by name.

The only answer was the rustling of trees in the soft night wind.

"He hasn't come back," said the boy. "What has happened to him ?"

"Perhaps he's gone home," suggested Cecil.

"No," replied Harry, "he has often told me that there is trouble enough there without his adding to it. It is a most mysterious thing."

"Then he's run away to sea," said Cecil, wearily.

"No ; Jack would not do that unless he had something very good to tempt him. Well, it's no use standing here—let's get into bed again."

They did so, and lay listening until they fell asleep.

When they awoke again all the boys were gathered together in the middle of the room, staring at Jack' bed.

The dummy was still there. He had not returned.

"What an awful thing !" said Bob. "He must have been very miserable to leave us in this way."

No answer was offered him, and Cecil Mead began to pull the dummy to pieces and put the bed in order.

"We've got to wait now until he is missed," he

said, 'and then you can all say what you like. None of you can say much, for you know—*nothing.*"

Jack Wyburn's disappearance amazed the greater part of the residents at Bangwell School It was, however, an open secret that he had resented his confinement to the house, and meant to set the command at defiance.

He had often done things " on principle " before, and if some of them were not exactly wise he at least showed that he had a will of his own.

Mr. Bangwell appeared to be much perturbed, and he went fully into the matter of Jack's recent movements, thereby acquiring a mass of information which may be termed Fact and Fiction combined.

This really left him exactly where he started, and he had to fall back upon the hypothesis of the boys that he had run away to sea.

He knew enough of Jack's home, of which we shall hear more of by-and-bye, to feel sure that he would not go there as a truant from school, and his first step was to communicate with the police.

This led to seeing some of the officials ; the schoolmaster wished the affair to be kept a secret, as it would, if known abroad, be detrimental to the school.

Through the aid of the officials telegrams were sent to all seaport towns, giving a description of Jack, and asking for him, if seen, to be detained until "his friends " came for him.

"His friends " was, of course, that one true friend to him, Mr. Bangwell, who made up his mind to give Jack, when he got him, such a tanning as he had never so much as dreamt of before.

There were especial reasons for Mr. Bangwell wishing to keep the knowledge of this presumed escapade from Jack's friends, and that made things all the more exasperating.

It was a harassing day for the boys.

None of them could do their work as it ought to have been done, and none of the teachers were in a frame of mind to be lenient.

The irritation felt by Mr. Bangwell descended to his assistants, and the cane was much in evidence, both in the morning and afternoon.

Poor Bob Rudge came in for half-a-dozen thrashings of varied duration, and the state of his countenance, grimy with dirt and tears, fully justified the cognomen of Smudge sometimes bestowed upon him by his chums.

"All right ; let 'em go on," he said, darkly, as he took his seat after the final "hoisting." "Something will come of it which they don't expect."

It was close upon five o'clock, and a few minutes later the boys were dismissed with a command that none of them were to stray from the playground.

"Pending news of Wyburn's whereabouts," said Mr. Bangwell, sternly, "all outside leave will be stopped."

There were low mutterings of, "What a beastly shame !" and other kindred and appropriate comments on this announcement.

Gloomy and savage, the boys walked into the playground where they gathered in groups discussing the state of things.

"Jack's done this on purpose to get us into trouble," said Ben Chicks ; "but it is just like him to go sneaking off in that way."

"Jack's no sneak," replied Harry Farnborough, hotly. " If he were here you dare not so much as whisper such a thing."

"So you think," growled

"So I *know*," said Harry, "and so we all know, and you may stare and frown at me as much as you please. I'm not afraid of you."

Ben turned away with a snarl from the group of which he and Harry formed a part, and sauntered off to the gate near which Ned Goran was standing.

These two fell into conversation together, which Harry Farnborough marked with some curiosity.

Hitherto, they had been anything but close companions, and now they appeared to be on the most friendly terms.

"I don't quite understand you two," muttered Harry, "surely you can't have put your heads together and— No *that's* impossible."

The group had now broken up, and Harry looking around him saw Bob Rudge going towards the house with the air of one who desired to escape observation.

For two or three days Bob's ways had been somewhat peculiar.

There was a mysterious aroma about his movements of the secret conspirator order. He had been very often absent from his fellows for half-an-hour at a time, and nobody knew whither he went.

He had certainly been questioned, but nothing came of that, owing to his having politely informed the querists that he " Would see them blowed first and then he would not tell them."

"He's off again," thought Harry. "Now I wonder what his game is?"

Except in fun, Harry would not have thought of playing the spy. On an occasion like this, he had no compunctions, for he looked upon Bob as a legitimate subject for the exercise of his love of the humorous.

So he quietly followed Bob into the house, and was just in time to see the flash of his legs as he hurried upstairs.

Harry was as light-footed as a fawn and silently followed. On reaching the head of the stairs he was fortunate enough to see Bob enter a room on tiptoe, about half-way down the corridor. Now this was a small chamber, sombre and cheerless, owing to its having only a borrowed light from a window in the corridor.

In the old days, when the place had been a single residence instead of a double one, the chamber had not been a room at all but a short passage leading to a bed-chamber.

In dividing the mansion the door of that chamber had been nailed up.

"Now what can he be doing there ?" thought Harry, as he crept up. "Perhaps he's got some white mice."

But it was not white mice or any class of animal pets that brought him there. He had simply come thither to work upon that old door, through which he or somebody else had previously made a small hole.

Harry saw him at work with a pocket-knife which he knew from experience to be as blunt as cheap knives generally are after a little use at school.

But he was getting along, for the old door was as rotten as wood could be, and yet held together.

The whole thing was instantly clear to the young spy.

What had been done to the fence outside Bob was doing to one of the nailed-up doors within.

There were at least half-a-dozen nailed-up doors about the place, but for the most part they were in positions where such an operation as Bob was now carrying on would have led to immediate discovery.

In that disused, and, except for lumber, almost useless room, Bob was practically safe from detection.

The idea of it tickled Harry immensely, and he resolved to wait a little and see the whole thing through.

Presently Bob stopped, and Harry, who had entered the room and was standing behind the door, saw that he had made a hole quite as big as an orange.

There was a pretty strong light on the other side, but what sort of apartment it was Harry could not see.

"Fanny!" said Bob, in a thrilling whisper.

There was a moment's silence, and then a door was heard to creak, and a soft footstep sounded in the adjoining room.

"Fanny!" said Bob again.

"Good gracious!" exclaimed a girlish voice. "What have you done?"

"I've made the hole bigger," replied Bob.

"How could you do it?"

"Easy," replied Bob. "The door is as soft as sponge cake. I could put my head throught it."

"I don't mean that," replied Fanny. "Of course I know it's rotten; but making so big a hole will lead to its being found out."

"They don't often come into the old lumber room," pleaded Bob.

"But they do sometimes," Fanny answered. "Besides, I don't see the sense of it."

"I do," said Bob."

"Well, what is the sense?"

"The hole is big enough now for me to—to put my face through and—and—*kiss you.*"

"Oh!" exclaimed Fanny, "what next, you impudent goose! Well, kiss me."

"I can't," said Bob, "if you stand so far off."

"Do you suppose that I'm coming up to you to be kissed?" returned Fanny. "What a creature I should be if I did!"

"Come a little nearer, then."

"Just a little then."

"Nearer."

"There; will that do?"

"You know it won't," gasped Bob, who had pressed his face close to the door and was struggling to get at his lady-love.

It was evidently a case of Tantalus—the fruit very near but not near enough to touch.

The little minx, whoever she was, was having a game with Bob.

"Surely you can reach me now?" she said.

"I—I can't," groaned Bob. "You're still two inches off."

"Poor old chap!" thought Harry, "he wants a little help. I've always been a friend to him, and I'll stand by him still."

Swiftly and silently he bore down upon Bob, who was in a stooping position, and gave him what elderly people call a violent push, and boys speak of as an unmerciful shove. Crash!

Bob's head went clean through the door, carrying before it a little cloud of rotten wood and dust.

Fanny shrieked with terror, and Harry heard her fall among a heap of boxes, some of which fell with a thunderous roar.

Cries were heard in the adjoining part of the house. "Pull your head back!" cried Harry, "or you'll have that old woman down on you"

Bob's only answer was a wriggle and a groan.

His head was fast.

Although the wood was so rotten it had broken in a somewhat jagged manner, and two or three pointed pieces pressed painfully upon his throat.

"Oh! my," gasped Harry; "here's a go. Give your head a jerk. It won't hurt you much."

But people when they have pointed things pressing on the jugular vein are apt to be gingerly in their movements. Thus it was with Bob.

He dare not budge.

And now there was a movement within the house that brought things to a climax.

Miss Fillwell, followed by half-a-dozen young ladies, hurriedly entered the room.

Fanny, a pretty dark-eyed and rather pert-looking girl of fourteen, had just risen to her feet.

"Oh! Miss Fillwell," she cried; "look at that horrid thing."

The horrid thing was Bob, and with unmeasured indignation he heard himself thus specified. But he said nothing. His eyes were fixed on Miss Fillwell.

She in turn looked at him as people look at some startling and novel phenomenon.

Bob's poll at first had to her the appearance of a head nailed to the door.

It was a ghastly sight.

But in a few moments she recovered herself, seeming to understand something of what had happened. and then she sprang upon him, and with a hand as flat and hard as an oval disc of wood, she gave him a box on the right ear, rapidly following it up with one on the left.

This was the stimulus he wanted, and pulling his head back with a jerk, he broke away the ragged, rotten wood and was free.

"You little villain!" said Miss Fillwell, through the hole. "I'll have you prosecuted for house-breaking."

But Bob and Harry had skedaddled off, and there was no response to the threat.

Failing in that direction she turned upon Fanny.

"Miss Whymper, you will have to undergo a course of punishment for your share in this outrage, and will begin with two hours of the backboard—go and lie down at once."

CHAPTER XI.

DISQUIETING RUMOURS.

MISS FILLWELL did did not write to Mr. Bangwell about the affair just described, but did a better thing, as far as her future peace was concerned.

She sent for the ironmonger and instructed him to cover the old door with a sheet of iron.

Thus was Bob Rudge cut off from secret communication with his lady-love. He was a kindred sufferer with Cobb ; but both were soon busy hatching fresh schemes for overcoming the obstacles to their wooing.

Two nights and a day passed and Jack did not return.

So it was whispered about Moatborough that one of the boys had run away " owing to cruel treatment."

The latter was not at first specified, but ingenious minds soon supplied what was wanted in that direction, and stories were soon in circulation which, if true, would have entitled Mr. Bangwell to penal servitude for life.

They said he had been keeping Jack " in a dark attic " without food for a week. He had also beaten him with " iron rods, tied him up by his thumbs," and so on.

In short, a " horror panic " was rising in the old town.

These things are like epidemics. Nobody knows their source or how they spread, and both are dangerous to the peace and safety of the victims.

Now on the second morning after Jack's disappearance, Mrs. Bangwell required a few things in the town, and, Cobb being busy, one of the boys was utilised as messenger.

This was often done, and the boys did not object to it, as a saunter about the town was at any time as good as sitting in that stuffy school.

The boy selected on this occasion was Cecil Mead. With a list of small things Mrs. Bangwell was in need of he started off, bent on making the most of his outing.

The High-street, as usual, was in a stagnant condition, very few people about and the shops looking as lively as the painted " flats " of a pantomime scene.

Cecil soon, however, marked one bright spot on the dull picture.

It was one of the prettiest, if not *the* prettiest, girl he had ever seen.

Although he had not set eyes on her before, he felt sure she was one of the pupils of Miss Fillwell's seminary.

She came out of a Berlin-wool shop, where she had probably been making purchases, judging by a small, limp-looking parcel she had in her hand.

She looked at Cecil, he glanced at her. There was a moment's hesitation on the part of both, and then he raised his cap.

" You belong to Mr. Bangwell's school ?" the girl said.

" Yes," replied Cecil, " and you—"

" Oh ! I am one of Miss Fillwell's pupils. We don't see much of each other, we girls and boys. It wouldn't be very proper."

" Well, I don't see what harm there would be, and it would be very nice."

The girl smiled, but somewhat sadly.

" One of your boys," she said, " has recently run away."

" It is said so," replied Cecil, " but some of us can't quite make up our minds to it."

" What has become of him, do you think ?"

" We don't know."

" Do—do you think Mr. Bangwell—has—killed him ?" asked the girl, hesitating.

" Goodness me—no !" exclaimed Cecil. " What put that into your head ?"

" There are such horrid stories about. I've just heard that Mr. Bangwell used to beat him with a wire whip."

" Oh ! that's bosh. We get licked occasionally, but that's not much."

And Cecil put on the air of one who has no fear of ordinary corporal punishment, for he wanted the pretty girl to look upon him as a brave lad.

It would have been all right if she had, for he had plenty of pluck, but the girl was not thinking of what he was then. It was Jack she had in her mind.

" I suppose," she said, after a pause, " that he will come *back* ?"

" Ah ! that's what we are all asking," Cecil said, " and nobody can find an answer."

" It wouldn't have mattered much if that horrid Ned Goran—" the girl began, and then stopped short, her face flushing.

" So you know Goran ?" exclaimed Cecil, opening his eyes.

" I know him because he's a *nuisance*," replied the girl, with flashing eyes

" A nuisance to you ?"

" Well, yes !"

" Then *I'll* put a stop to it," said Cecil, gallantly.

" You had better do nothing," returned the girl, hurriedly ; " he would only— Never mind what he would do. It doesn't matter. You are to do nothing to him. He is not *worth* it. I must go now."

She walked off a pace or two, and, stopping, looked round.

" If you should hear anything of Jack Wyburn," she said—"anything worth hearing, you might let me know."

" How ?" asked Cecil.

"Write it on a slip of paper and toss it over the fence any morning just before nine o'clock. I shall get it."

" What name shall I address it to ?" asked Cecil.

But the girl had gone on quickly, and speedily vanished out of sight.

" She knows Jack's name and Goran's too," muttered Cecil, as he strolled on. " Now, I wonder how that come about? Something's been going on which *I* know nothing about. On my word, she's the prettiest girl I've ever seen."

Cecil, without being ultra-susceptible, was inclined to be sensitive to a pretty face, and the one he had just looked on set him thinking.

He was so wrapped up in the pleasing subject that he did not see Gruesum, who was approaching from the opposite direction, the worse for drink, and swaggering along.

He was advancing in a direct line towards Cecil, and doggedly refused to turn aside. Cecil, as we have said, was too busy thinking to see him, and thus a collision between them was brought about.

———

CHAPTER XII.

GRUESUM AND CECIL—LETTING IN THE LIGHT—A
DANGEROUS EXPEDITION.

"NOW, then, where are you coming to, you school brat?" said Gruesum.

He aimed a blow at Cecil.

The youngster avoided it easily, for the ruffian, though heavy handed, was slow in his movements. Backing into the street Cecil began to chaff him.

"You are a brave fellow," he said. "Why don't you fight a man? Have you seen Sam Barlow lately?"

The name of Barlow was to Gruesum what a red rag is to a bull. He began to foam and plunged about in a vain effort to get hold of Cecil, who, as the saying goes, "walked round him," laughed at his vain attempt to strike him.

How long this sort of fun would have gone on is not easy to say, for Cecil was quite ready for half an hour of it and Gruesum in his fury would not have given in. But it was suddenly put a stop to by the appearance of Mike Feeley on the scene.

The old man came running across the road with an activity one would hardly have expected from one of his years, and seized Gruesum by the arm.

"What are you doing, you mad fool?" he hissed in his ear.

Cecil, who had drawn aside and was watching the pair closely, saw that, strong as Gruesum was, he was held fast in the grip of the old sexton, who must have possessed muscles of steel.

"What am I doing?" roared Gruesum. "I want just to *get at another of 'em.*"

"There! that will do; get away," said Feeley, pushing him away from Cecil. "You've been drinking, as usual, and I tell you THAT IT WON'T DO NOW!"

The pair disappeared down one of the narrow turnings in the street, and Cecil strolled on in a very serious mood.

Some of the words he had just heard set him thinking.

"He wants to get at another of us," was his mental comment. "Another! What does that mean? Has he already got at one of us, *and that one Jack Wyburn?*"

A new light had broken in upon Jack's disappearance, revealing all sorts of dreadful possibilities. But what was there to get hold of for action in the matter?

Cecil was trying to think out this part of the subject when he felt a finger lightly laid upon him.

Turning, he saw a ragged boy just behind him.

"Excuse me," said the boy, "I didn't mean to be rude. Will you please come up this passage and speak to me?"

"Who are you?" asked Cecil, doubtfully. He had heard of boys being decoyed up into places to be murdered, and Jack's recent disappearance, in the light of what he had heard, gave colour to all sorts of suppositions.

"My name is Daniel Foster," replied the boy, "and Buck Gruesum is my father. He ill-treats me, and a friend of yours interfered with him the other day when he was beating me."

"I heard Jack Wyburn speak of it," said Cecil.

"Yes; that's his name," replied the boy, eagerly "It's about him I want to talk."

"All right," said Cecil. "I'll hear what you have to say. But no tricks."

"Do I look as if I could play any tricks with you," asked Daniel Foster. "I'm so badly fed that I haven't the strength of a rat, and you are tall and strong."

"You speak better than most ragged boys," said Cecil, as they turned into a narrow court; "how's that?"

"Father was a very respectable man, and gave me some education," replied the boy, "and mother teaches me now."

"Oh! that's it. Well, what have you to say to me?" asked Cecil.

"Jack Wyburn is—is—missing, isn't he?" said Dan, lowering his voice.

"Yes; he is."

"Do you know where he is gone?"

"No; I wish I did. Nobody does."

"I don't know either," said Dan; "but I can guess that something happened to him, and I believe Buck Gruesum is in it."

"What makes you think *that?*" asked Cecil, with a startled look on his face.

"Because he's been hinting that he got level with *one* of you," said Dan. "He's been on the drink the last two days, and has been more like some wild beast than a man. He goes out at night too, and he and Mike Feeley are always together."

"But all this is mere guess work," said Cecil. "We can do nothing."

"I think if Buck Gruesum were watched at night something would come of it," said Dan.

"Well, can't you do it?"

"No; he locks mother and me in the house, and he says he will murder us if we so much as look out after dark.. So I was thinking that if you were to speak to the schoolmaster something could be done. But you mustn't speak of me. If Buck thought I'd so much as whispered a word to you he'd torture me first and then kill me as he does cats and rabbits."

"What a blackguard he is!"

"He's a brute!"

"I don't know what to say to you," said Cecil; "but I thank you for giving me a clue—"

"He was so kind to me," said Dan, "and his friend, too. I will never forget them."

"Yes; quite right. I'll have a talk with my friends over what you've told me," said Cecil, "and we will see what can be done."

He put his hand into his pocket to see if he had any money to give the poor half-starved boy; but Dan drew back.

"No," he said, "I don't want anything for telling you this. I would rather not be paid for it."

"But you are hungry?"

"That's nothing. I'm always hungry."

And to cut short all further discussion he hurried away.

It is almost needless to say that Cecil went back

to the school in a very troubled frame of mind. If he had perceived any definite ground to work upon he could have gone to Mr. Bangwell at once and enlisted his services ; but with only a few vague hints from a ragged boy he felt that nothing could come of it.

At the same time he felt that there was good cause for thinking that Jack had met with foul play.

The bare idea of his having been murdered made Cecil grind his teeth and breathe a vow of vengeance, for between him and Jack a strong friendship existed up to the time of the latter's disappearance.

Before doing anything he decided to consult with Harry Farnborough and one or two others.

Accordingly a Council of Enquiry, as it was called, was held at noon, of which Cecil, Harry, Tom Drake, and Bob Rudge were the principal members.

First they wanted to know what the hints of Dan Foster were worth.

If of any value what could be done to utilise them ?

And if anything could be done, who was to do it ?

"I think the first thing to be done," said Harry Farnborough, "is to find out where that ruffian Gruesum goes at night."

"Ah ! yes," said Cecil. "At night—an awkward time for us."

"Jack got out—so could somebody else."

"Just so ; but we are not all like Jack."

"Look here," said Bob Rudge, " I'll go."

"You ?" replied Harry. "A pretty mess you would make of it. If anybody is to venture it must be Cecil or me. Where does Gruesum live ?"

"In an alley behind Peddle the hatter's shop," said Tom Drake. "I heard him making a row there one day."

CHAPTER XIII.

HARRY AND CECIL HAVE SOME EXPERIENCE OF NIGHT PROWLING—GRUESUM AND FEELEY—A QUICK RUN HOME.

THEN that is our starting-point," said Harry. "Now, Cecil, which of us is to run the risk of a night out. Shall we toss for it ?"

"Why not both go ?" suggested Tom Drake.

"Ah ! that's the idea," said Bob Rudge, and for once everybody agreed with him. So it was settled. Cecil and Harry were to get away when the house was at rest and do their best to learn something of the fate of their missing friend. A general impression now rested on the boys that Jack was dead.

With gloomy feelings the council, after being individually bound to secrecy, broke up, and with heavy, anxious hearts awaited the coming of the night.

Cecil, meanwhile, tried to get another glimpse of the very pretty girl he had met in the High-street, of whom, by the way, he said nothing to his chums.

The fact is Cecil was rather hard hit, and had, in his boyish way, tumbled into love. He was induced to think that she did not take such an interest in Jack without very strong reasons, and a feeling akin to jealousy took possession of him. But he shook it off, exclaiming—

"Hang it all ! Jack's a brick, and I don't wonder at the girl being spoons on him."

He and Harry decided to take stout sticks with them as a means of defence in case of an attack upon them, and it must be confessed that as the time for them to go upon their expedition drew near, their pulses beat a little faster. Harry Farnborough, after carefully reconnoitring the premises, came to the conclusion that the best way out was by the scullery door, which was secured by bolts only.

They could get out of the grounds by way of the back garden, which was bordered by a lane leading into the town.

The old trick of dummying Jack's bed was to be repeated in duplicate in the beds of the two young adventurers.

It was a horribly risky thing they were about to attempt, but it was for the sake of a dear friend, and whatever happened they felt that their consciences would be free.

"It isn't as if we were sneaking out to do anything wrong," said Harry.

Night came at last, and the various branches of the household settled in turns to rest.

The dummies in the beds were another success, and when Mr. Philpot had gone his rounds Harry and Cecil came out from under their couches and prepared to start.

A whispered "Good luck to you !" passed round the dormitory, and then Harry softly opened the door and listened.

The house was absolutely still, and as dark as the black-hole of Calcutta.

Each had a pair of boots in his hand, and together they began to grope along the corridor to the stair-case.

"Ugh !" suddenly exclaimed Cecil.

"Hush !" whispered Harry.

"Something rubbed against my leg."

"It's only the cat ; she's been at me. Don't be nervous !"

"I'm not nervous, but terribly excited."

Down the stairs they went, step by step, every slight creaking of the stairs giving their hearts an upward bound.

The hall was reached, and bearing round to the right, they proceeded along the passage.

Suddenly a fearful snort fell upon their ears.

"Good Heavens !" gasped Cecil ; "what is that ?"

"Biffins snoring," replied Harry ; "we are near his room. That's the start. Now he's going right away."

Which Biffins was doing, giving out the most agonising board-scraping, plate-scratching, man-choking sounds ever heard.

As soon as they were past his door Harry brought out from his pocket a box of matches and struck a light.

By its aid they easily made their way to the scullery-door.

Then they stood for a few moments on the mat to pull on their boots. Cecil softly drew back the bolts, and they were in the open air.

"Whew !" said Cecil, softly ; "so far all's well."

"Do be quiet," replied Harry, testily ; "somebody will be sure to hear us. Hush ! What noise is that ?"

They stood quite still, but could hear nothing. Harry was under the impression that he had heard a movement overhead, at one of the windows, or on the tiles, but he now felt sure he was mistaken.

Outside it was starlight, and they could see the outline of the garden-paths. Choosing the centre one, they softly and quickly traversed it to the hedge at the bottom.

It was a combination of holly and thorn, and not by any means easy to get through; but they found a hole near the ground, through which they crept.

They were now in the lane, and stopped to breathe a moment.

Hark! What is that?

A bell!

The bell of the school, rung by no gentle hand.

Clash—clash! as if rung by a terrified man.

At that hour, and in that place, an appalling sound.

"Who's ringing that bell now?" asked Harry Farnborough between his teeth.

"It can't be Jack, anyhow," said Cecil.

"The fools—the asses—to play such a prank to-night! It will ruin all."

"I've an idea, Harry."

"Oh! hang your ideas."

"Don't be savage about nothing. It was one of Chicks' lot who rang the bell before."

"That won't help us now. Thank goodness it's stopped."

"There are lights moving about the house."

"Of course, and all the beds will be examined."

And they groaned aloud.

"Hush!" said Cecil, "somebody's bawling in the playground."

Crouching down beside the fence they clearly heard the voice of a man, presumably a policeman, bawling out—

"House there! Is it a real alarm or the old game?"

Somebody was heard to say something in reply. Harry judged it was Mr. Bangwell speaking from an upper window, but as it was on the other side of the house it was difficult to truly tell.

What was said was not at all clear, but the rejoinder was plainly heard.

"You will have to stop this sort of thing, somehow, sir, or there will be trouble."

Retreating footsteps followed, the window was heard to close, a light or two floated about for a few moments, and then all in the house was dark and still again.

"They haven't found out anything about us," said Harry, recovering his spirits.

"Dummies for ever!" softly returned Cecil.

"We have no time to lose!" said Harry; "let us get away to Gruesum's house."

"Taking good care to dodge the night police-men," added Cecil.

This was absolutely essential, for the boys walking abroad at that hour would naturally excite the attention of any official on duty, and then they would be stopped and questioned.

It would not do to be seen, for then their plan of watching Gruesum would fail.

The residence of this worthy has already been sufficiently indicated.

Five minutes' quick walking brought the boys within a short distance of it, and getting into a dark doorway which commanded a view of the house, they begun their watch.

"How do you feel?" softly whispered Cecil.

"Not very rosy," replied Harry.

"Just like a burglar, eh?"

"Something in that way."

A few minutes elapsed, and the sense of discomfort increased upon them. They began to think, as anyone in their fear might have done, that they had come upon a fool's errand and had better go back to bed again.

Harry, indeed, was about to suggest it when the door of Gruesum's house opened, and the ruffian came forth.

They could see that he had a short stick in one hand, and a dark lantern in the other.

Tucking the stick under his arm he locked the door, and then, to the amazement of the boys, sat down upon the ground.

A reason for this movement was made apparent by his drawing out of his pocket a thick pair of socks, which he drew over his boots.

"He's going to do something bad to-night," thought Harry.

He passed his arm through Cecil's, and they stood quite still, their hearts going the pace; but, otherwise, they were quiet enough.

Gruesum having got the socks on got up, and with a stealthy, panther-like step bore down upon the main street.

He passed so close to the boys that they could have put out their hands and touched him; but he did not suspect the presence of anyone, and passed on.

Harry, peeping out, saw him, when he reached the main street, look up and down, and then hurry across the roadway.

"Come on!" said Harry, in a stage whisper. "We mustn't lose sight of him."

But when they got to the main street they found that he had disappeared.

And, what made things so aggravating, there was at least half-a-dozen turnings on the opposite side, down any of which he might have gone.

It was also true they were for the most part mere courts and alleys, of which the boys knew little, and any attempt to get upon his trail seemed hopeless.

"Perhaps he's gone to commit a burglary?" said Cecil.

"If he has, I hope he will get caught," replied Harry. "Suppose we go quietly down the street, keeping close in the shadow of the houses?"

It was the custom in Moatborough, as it is in many country towns, to turn off the gas at a certain hour, leaving the whole place in darkness, and as the boys crept out into the High-street the moment for this to be done had arrived.

Somebody did the job by turning it off at the main at the town-hall, and Cecil and Harry, not acquainted with the custom, were considerably staggered by the sudden disappearance of the lights up and down the street.

"Who's trick is that?" gasped Cecil.

"Something gone wrong at the gasworks, I suppose," replied Harry, "and it is a fortunate thing for us. We can safely pry about now."

"Hist!" whispered Cecil, "somebody's on the other side of the street."

It was very dark, but the boys drawing back close against the shutters of a shop could just discern two men moving stealthily along on the opposite side of the road.

THE
BANGWELL BOYS
BEING THE SEQUEL TO
Hardiboy James ; or, Chums and Chappies.

"Don't you mock me! cried Gruesum, raising his stick with a threatening air. "You know very well what I mean."

No. 15.   Price One Penny.

They made no noise, but the youthful watchers were not alarmed. They did not think of ghosts, having at once recognised Buck Gruesum as one of the wayfarers.

In the other, after looking closely, they recognised Mike Feeley the sexton.

They did not go far, no farther than the gate of the churchyard of St. Peter's, which Mike Feeley opened with exceeding care, and let himself and his companion in.

The boys were now in a state of growing excitement. They would have been more than boys if they had been anything else. A few hurried words were exchanged.

"Perhaps they are going to dig *a grave?*" whispered Harry.

"Or fill up one," answered Cecil.

"Shall we go over and see?"

"Yes."

With light footsteps they made their way to the gate, which had been left open, and cautiously peered into the churchyard.

It looked very black, and they could see nothing.

Nor could they hear a sound.

There was no indication of either pick or spade being used, not the faintest sound of any movement.

"They're gone," said Harry.

"Where?" cried Cecil.

"Ah! that's the question."

St. Peter's Churchyard was closely hemmed in on three sides by houses, so that the way in was of necessity the way out. Harry suggested he and Cecil should hide on the opposite side and await the return of the two men.

"Perhaps they will talk," he said, "and let out something?"

Cecil could suggest nothing better to do, for the idea of blundering about in a dark churchyard to find two dangerous men was not all to his taste.

So they crossed the road and got into another doorway, and all might have gone well, but for the untoward coming of a watcher of the night.

The heavy footsteps of an approaching policeman were heard long before he was in sight, and the safest thing for the boys to do was to clear out at once.

But they lingered until he was dangerously near, and then endeavoured to get away unseen.

Ill luck attended them.

Cecil tripped over a raised piece of pavement and fell.

"Who's there?" demanded the policeman, turning on his lantern.

"Up and run, Cecil!" said Harry, hurriedly.

Cecil had bruised his knees rather extensively, but he got up and ran as hard as he could.

Harry, who could easily have gone on ahead and left him, kept by his side.

"Stop thief!" cried the policeman.

He blew his whistle, and it was almost immediately answered in two directions.

To keep in the High-street was to court arrest.

So Harry dived into one of the side thoroughfares, and by keeping his head clear, was able to work his way, by sundry narrow, and, in some cases, unsavoury routes, back to the school, Cecil following.

They got through the hole in the fence, reached the kitchen door, whipped off their boots, and entered the house.

Harry quickly bolted the door, and then they stood panting for a minute or so, not daring to go upstairs until their breathing was easier.

At length they went forward, groping their way in the dark, and knowing pretty well where to go, safely arrived at the bottom of the staircase.

Harry convulsively clutched the arm of his chum.

"What's the matter?" Cecil asked.

"Go on," said Harry, in a hoarse, low tone.

Cecil hastened upstairs, and Harry followed.

They reached the dormitory, and, Cecil having got the door open, passed in.

Harry followed, and a moment later struck a light, using one of the matches he carried.

"There's a bolt to the door, Cecil," he said shivering; "draw it."

"You looked scared, Harry. What's the matter?"

"Draw the bolt, I say—that's it. Now you've a piece of candle in your box. Get it out."

He struck another match, and Cecil having got out the piece of candle, it was lighted.

The boys were all sound asleep.

"Now, old man," said Cecil, "you've had a scare. What was it?"

"Why, this," said Harry as he began to pull off his clothes. "*Somebody was walking about in the hall below.*"

"Oh! murder," gasped Cecil, "you must have fancied it."

"No, I didn't," returned Harry, "and I heard whoever it was breathing. I never had such a turn in my life, and I don't want another. We can't talk about it now. Let us jump into bed and get to sleep."

CHAPTER XIV.

AN OPPORTUNE HALF-HOLIDAY — STARTLING APPEARANCE OF SAM BARLOW—THE BELLS AGAIN.

WHEN the morning came there was no small talk among the boys about the ringing of the bell. As before, it had been a short, sharp performance — a "run-away" ring on a big scale.

Mr. Bangwell was very much exasperated, and his temper was not at all improved by a visit from a court officer with a summons for "ringing a certain bell at night to the disturbance of her Majesty's subjects of the town of Moatborough."

Now, this summons did the friends of Jack Wyburn a good turn. It put an end to the restriction upon their liberty.

"I have hitherto," said Mr. Bangwell, "considered the town of Moatborough, by keeping the boys at home as much as possible; but it is clear that Moatborough does not consider me. It is a half-holiday to-day. The boys will be free to go where they please, within a boundary of two miles."

This was joyous news to the particular friends of

the missing boy; all of whom were, of course, fully enlightened about the result of the midnight expedition.

A hasty consultation was held, and they resolved to devote the afternoon to their lost friend, by endeavouring to solve the mystery of his fate.

They divided themselves into two parties, of whom one consisted of Harry Farnborough, Cecil Mead, Bob Rudge, and Tom Drake.

As we shall follow this party we need not specify the others by name.

Acting according to a plan arranged, they set out as soon as dinner was finished, and quietly made their way to the churchyard of St. Peter's. Their object was to seek evidence of somebody having recently been interred there.

It was a very curious church, and with two or three odd narrow places at the back, where nobody scarcely ever went.

From the boys' point of view one of these would be just the place for Mike Feeley to hide the remains of a foe.

It was a crude idea, but our boys were not endowed with all the experience and acuteness of a detective force, as some of the heroes of certain writers are, and they may be pardoned if they went on what looked like a wild-goose chase, especially as it was the means of bringing about their object.

On getting together in the churchyard they began the search, and headed by Harry Farnborough, went behind the time-eaten, weather-beaten building.

There a high, blank wall stood, about twelve feet from the church, forming a long, narrow, blind passage, down which was a single row of graves, with all sorts of strange tombstones, the youngest a century old, from which all records of the dead had long been washed away.

"What a ghastly hole!" said Bob Rudge. "I don't see that any digging has been done there."

"We can't see unless we go right to the bottom," replied Harry Farnborough.

They walked on together, all imbued with a sense of the uncanniness of the spot, and had got about half-way down, when a man suddenly appeared at the further end.

To Bob Rudge it seemed as if he had sprung from the ground, and the general feeling of all was that of being startled by a half-expected apparition.

Their first impulse was to turn and run, but it was dispelled by Bob's exclamation of—

"Why, it's Sam Barlow, the bell-ringer!"

So it was, and he was every whit as much surprised as they were, and came hurrying up to them, looking very stern.

"What are you prowling about here for?" he asked.

"We don't mind telling you," replied Harry. "We are looking for our friend Jack Wyburn, whom we believe to have been murdered."

In a few words he told Sam about their adventure on the previous night, and the theory they had drawn from it.

At the idea of Jack's being buried in the churchyard Sam faintly smiled.

"No," he said; "your friend isn't buried in the churchyard. Feeley would never run the risk of that; but, for all that, the poor lad, if he is murdered, may not be far away. There's plenty of room for him *under the church.*"

"Where?" exclaimed the boys.

"Under the church," repeated Sam. "There's a lot of passages and vaults, running in every direction. Fifty corpses could be put away and yet room left for more."

He was quiet for a moment, and then, with a very serious face, went on.

"I believe you young gentlemen could keep a secret if you were trusted with it?"

"Oh! yes—yes," they chorussed.

"Then I'll let you into one," said Sam. "There's a way into the vaults known to nobody but me. I've just come out of it, and if you've got the heart in you, we'll all go down and search the place together."

Of course they said they would go. It would be an adventure if nothing came of it, so Sam, after binding them to secrecy, led the way to the bottom end of the passage and stopped against the last buttress of the church.

On one side of it was a slab of stone, which looked as if it were a solid part of the building; but Sam, taking a small crowbar from his pocket, placed it between the slab and the main wall, and prized it out.

It was only about four inches thick, and as it fell it disclosed an opening big enough to admit the body of a man.

"I'll go first," said Sam. "Don't be afraid. It's dark, but there's daylight further on."

Inside the opening was a flight of dilapidated stone steps, down which the party, one by one, descended.

It was not quite dark at the bottom, but looked very black ahead.

"Catch hold of each other's hands and follow me," said Sam. "You needn't be afraid. There's no wells to fall down."

They crept along, the boys breathlessly silent, until Sam, having traversed about a dozen yards, called upon them to stop.

They then heard him draw back a bolt and a door was thrown open.

Beyond was a dimly lighted chamber, with shelves on the opposite side filled with coffins.

"This," said Sam, "is an old family vault long out of use, and nobody ever comes here now. Mister Feeley long ago broke open all the coffins and took away what there was to steal."

"Ugh—the brute!" ejaculated Harry.

"Oh! yes," said Sam, "he's a nice old man, he is—but he's cunning, and nothing can be brought home to him. Now we'll try this end. There's a passage running right up to the altar, with branches on each side. There may be a place there where a body might be hidden."

The passage he referred to was lighted by small apertures at regular distances in the roof. Sam explained to the boys that they were in the chief aisle above, close to the pews, and not observable by occasional visitors to the church. On the right and left were four or five unglazed windows, and beyond them were what Sam called, "the cells."

"You take the right side and I'll take the left," he said. "We shall then see if anybody is here."

It was in the very first one they came to that the boys saw a startling and terrifying sight.

As they reached the window, they beheld their friend Jack lying at full length upon the ground, securely bound with ropes, and apparently dead.

Running about .ne dismal chamber were a number of rats, materially adding to the horrors of the scene.

A simultaneous cry from the boys drew Sam Barlow's attention to the spot, and he, coming over hurriedly, peered in.

"Save us !" he cried. "There he is."

The boys were so overcome that they could do nothing ; but Sam, made of sterner stuff, rushed to a door near the window, and, drawing back two outside bolts, darted in.

In a few minutes he was outside with Jack in his arms.

"He's not dead," he gasped ; "but he's only just alive. Go on, up the stairs—that way. It leads to near the belfry."

Refusing all help he carried the form of Jack alone, and with eager steps and panting breath the boys hurried on by the way he pointed out.

By a door they entered the church, close to the belfry, which was open.

"Lay hold of the ropes and *ring*," cried Sam. "We'll have plenty witnesses to what's been done here. RING ! RING !"

CHAPTER XV.

MIKE FEELEY GETS A SHAKING—JACK'S SERIOUS CONDITION—SAM BARLOW IN A FIX.

SUCH a jangling and a clanging Moatborough in all its experience of bells had never heard before. Stragglers sauntering about stopped short, and gazing around them asked what it all meant, children paused in their play, tradesmen came hurrying to their doors.

"It isn't Sam Barlow now," said one. "He's got the sack, and the key of the belfry's been taken from him. Ah ! there goes Mike Feeley, mad with rage. It's the Bangwell Boys again."

Yes, there was the old sexton, looking like an infuriated hobgoblin, tearing along to the church with a bunch of keys in his hand.

In an opposite direction, the vicar, a tall, handsome man of fifty, was also hurrying thither, and bent on stopping for good and all the unseemly ringing of the bells.

They met at the churchyard gate, exchanged a few hasty words, and with a little crowd, among whom was a policeman, hurried to the belfry-tower.

"Clang—clang, jangle—jangle !" went the bells.

Mike Feeley, with trembling hands thrust the key into the lock, turned it, and threw open the door.

At first he only saw four boys pulling madly at the ropes, and was about to rush upon them, when he caught sight of Sam Barlow, with the insensible Jack Wyburn in his arms.

He stopped short, and, staggering back, leant gasping against the wall.

The angry vicar pressed forward, and close behind him was a policeman. The rest of the people gathered round the door garping in.

The boys stopped ringing, and the ropes, without hands, danced up and down, twisting this way and that like so many serpents in agony.

"What is the meaning of this outrage ?" demanded the vicar. "Stand ! all of you. Officer, see that none of these boys escape."

"We are not going to run away, sir," replied Harry Farnborough. "We rang to bring somebody here."

The vicar now for the first time saw Sam and his burden, and stared, as well he might, at so strange a spectacle. The rope bonds were still around the form of the insensible boy.

"It's the lost young gentleman from the school," said Sam. "We found 'im in the vaults. He's nigh on dead, sir."

"Found him—in the vaults !" exclaimed the wondering vicar, "who put him there ?"

"Ask Mike Feeley," cried Sam, pointing a finger at the sexton. "He and his friend, Buck Gruesum know all about it."

"I know—know nothing !" shrieked the old sexton. "I ain't been down in the vaults these six months."

"We'll see about that," said Sam, resolutely ; "but we won't waste time talking here." Turning to the vicar, he went on— "We want a doctor, sir. The poor boy is as nigh dead as he can be."

"A marvellous—strange business," muttered the vicar. "Bring him along. Some of you help Barlow. Untie those ropes, they seem to be cutting into his flesh. Carry him to the Greyhound Inn, and one of you run for Doctor Grece."

The policeman pulled out a knife, and having severed the cords around and about poor Jack, helped Sam Barlow to carry him out.

The boys followed, with the vicar immediately behind, and the wondering crowd parted to let them pass.

Mike Feeley drew back a few inches, but did not budge any further. As Sam passed he fixed his eyes upon him with the most malevolent look ever seen on the face of man.

The Greyhound was just opposite the church, and the landlord was standing by the door, waiting to see what was the cause of the commotion.

When he saw an apparently dead body being brought into his house he seemed about to offer a protest, but, catching the eye of the vicar, touched his hat, and said—

"An accident, sir, I suppose. Them boys ought not to play at bell-ringing."

"The boy is hurt," said the vicar ; "but not in the way you suppose. I believe you have a sofa in your bar-parlour ?"

"Yes, sir."

"Then, with your leave, we will place him there until Doctor Grece has examined him. You can let these young gentlemen in, but nobody else. By the way, one of you boys had better go for Mr. Bangwell."

Harry Farnborough volunteered for this duty and sped away. The rest followed their friend into the bar parlour.

"He breathes," said the vicar, bending over Jack; "but that is all. Good Heaven! how starved and pinched he looks. A horrible, most dastardly outrage has been committed here!"

"Shall I give him a little brandy, sir?" asked the landlord.

"A few drops will not hurt him in any case," replied the vicar.

Jack's teeth were clenched together, and had to be forced apart ere the potent liquor could be administered.

The vicar administered it by drops, and the effect was soon visible. Jack began to shiver and half-opened his eyes.

"Drink a little more, my poor boy," implored the vicar. "There, that is right. Now you are better."

Jack's eyes were open now, but he did nothing beyond staring about him. He showed no signs of recognising anyone in the room.

CHAPTER XVI.

A MOMENTOUS QUESTION.

JACK'S school chums were deeply affected, and the eyes of all there were filled with tears. Bob stepped forward, and in a choking voice said—

"Jack—Jack! you know me, don't you?"

But Jack did not so much as turn his eyes in Bob's direction. He only stared like a figure of stone.

And now Dr. Grece appeared on the scene and went to work upon the patient.

He asked a question or two, got at the main facts, and then ran his hands over his body.

"There are no bones broken," he said. "It is a case of exhaustion arising from exposure and lack of nourishment. You have been giving him brandy, I perceive. Let him have a little more. In a case of this description it is an excellent servant."

A little more brandy was given to Jack, and then there were some signs of returning intelligence in his eyes. He turned his head about, looking at those around him in a puzzled way.

"He is coming round," now said the doctor, "but he won't get over this affair just yet. How do you do, ir?"

It was Mr. Bangwell, excited and alarmed, who had just come into the room.

He returned the doctor's greeting, and turned to Jack.

"What a horrible thing," he said. "One of my most promising pupils. Poor boy—poor boy!"

"I have heard—indirectly," said the vicar—"that he ran away from school."

"He did," replied Mr. Bangwell; "but why he should do so I cannot tell."

"Perhaps the poor boy will be able to explain?"

"I hope and trust he will. I have nothing to fear."

Mr. Bangwell spoke in a quiet, dignified manner, that did much to dispel the suspicions of the boy having been ill-treated, entertained at first by the vicar.

He had heard some of the idle rumours afloat, and not knowing the schoolmaster, had, of course, become prejudiced against him.

In addition to the brandy, Dr. Grece administered another restorative, which had the effect o bringing Jack to consciousness.

He made an effort to speak, but his voice was reduced to a faint whisper.

"Not yet, my lad," said the doctor, kindly; "by-and-bye will be soon enough for you to talk. We must get you to bed without delay."

"Can he be taken back to the school?" asked Mr. Bangwell.

"Yes, I think so," replied the doctor; "but he will need the best of nursing."

"He shall have it," replied Mr. Bangwell. "My boys are well taken care of at all times. You are welcome to examine them on this point if it pleases you."

Mr. Bangwell was somewhat nettled by the rather constrained air of the vicar and the doctor, shrewdly guessing the cause—and he had a right to be so.

An open carriage was obtained, and Jack, having had another restorative, was carried to it.

The doctor and Mr. Bangwell accompanied him.

The boys were left behind with Sam Barlow, to accompany the police officer to the station, and explain the facts of the discovery to the inspector.

"I mean that Mike Feeley to get a lifer for this," said Sam Barlow, on their way. "He ought to hang, but that can't be done, as the young gentleman isn't dead."

At the police-station Sam and the boys received a rude shock. In a calm, official way the inspector put a few questions to Sam.

"You led these young gentlemen to where the body was lying?"

"Yes, sir."

"Through the belfry door."

"Oh! no, sir. That was locked, and that's the reason why we couldn't get out."

"But," asked the inspector, fixing an eagle glance upon Sam, "*how did you get in?*"

"Well, to tell the truth," said Sam, "it was by a way known only to myself."

"And have you been there lately?"

"Yes, sir, I was there just before the young gentlemen came up, and—"

"Stop!" said the inspector. "I wish to warn you against saying anything more, for whatever you tell me *will be used against you.*"

Sam stared at him aghast.

This was for him a totally unexpected turn of affairs.

Not for one moment had either one of the boys thought that anybody but Mike Feeley and Buck Gruesum would be implicated in the business.

"I ought to tell you," continued the inspector,

"that it is possible that the young gentleman who has been victimised may be able to clear you from all suspicion. I hope so, I am sure, but meanwhile I must detain you here."

"You can't do it," cried Sam Barlow, hoarsely; "it isn't right."

The inspector made a sign, and two officers standing behind strode up, one on each side of the dismayed Sam.

"Now, Barlow, take things quietly," said the inspector, calmly; "it may be all right, you know. In that case you won't be detained long, and you will be treated well here."

"Here," repeated Sam—"a prisoner, like a thief! I've got a wife and child."

"Ah! my friend, you haven't always thought of them when on the drink."

Sam's head sank upon his breast.

"Heaven forgive me!" he muttered; "it's a punishment for me. I've made too good a friend of the drink."

"As for you, young gentlemen," said the inspector, "you need not remain. I will let you know when your evidence is wanted."

In a dreamy state the three boys left the police-station, and outside they stood still for a few moments staring at each other.

"Could Barlow have done it?" asked Cecil Mead.

"I don't know," groaned Tom Drake. "Let us get away from here. I've had enough outing for one day."

Jack, meanwhile, had been got safely back to school. Each moment he seemed better; but he was in a very sad state of weakness.

That he would have a very terrible tale to tell was certain, but for the present he was not allowed to go into particulars.

One question was, however, permitted by the doctor.

Indeed, it was at his instigation that it was asked.

"Do you know your assailant? Can you tell us who placed you where your friends found you?"

And Jack, with a shake of the head, answered—

"No, I cannot; indeed, I do not know."

CHAPTER XVII.

JACK GETS BETTER AND TELLS HIS STORY—SAM BARLOW TURNS OVER A NEW LEAF.

THE majority of the boys had been right away into the country, and knew nothing of the events of the day. But on their return they found someone ready waiting at the gates to impart the astonishing news.

This person was Cobb, who was in a state of bursting excitement, such as no horrible event had ever thrown him into before. It had the effect of strong drink upon him. His face flushed, his eyes stood out of his head, his whole form trembled.

"They've found Master Wyburn," he said, "church vault—s'rounded by coffins—millions of rats—Sam Barlow the murderer. Oh! it is a go!"

The buzz of excitement increased in the playground, until Mr. Philpot came out and begged the boys to be quiet, as Jack had fallen into an easy sleep. "The doctor says he must not be disturbed by anything," the usher said. The boys acquiesced in the desire for quietude, but did it with an ill grace. Ned Goran, who thought himself a little more than a boy, and Ben Chicks made some sneering remarks about "shamming," that excited the ire of Bob Rudge.

"Shamming!" said Bob, indignantly. "There's precious little of that about him. He don't go about gammoning people."

"What do you mean by that, you little beast?" said Ned Goran.

"Beast yourself," said Bob, keeping just out of arm's reach; "while my meaning is this, that he doesn't pretend as if butter wouldn't melt in his mouth, and in secret do all sorts of things that are wrong."

"What wrong?" demanded Chicks.

"Oh! I know more about you than you think," returned Bob. "Do you know The Two Scullers, down by the river? Nice house and nice company for boys."

"I'll twist your neck if I get hold of you," growled Ben.

"But you haven't got hold of me yet," replied Bob, as he dodged the extended arm of Ben, and ran away.

Before the boys went to bed that night they learnt that Jack had awakened much refreshed from his sleep, and been able to take nourishment. The doctor was not coming again until morning.

It was a very still evening for the boys, but in the kitchen there was a slight disturbance, owing to Cobb's attempting to act what he called "The Drammy of the Church Wall; or, the Missing 'Ero Found."

In the first act, portraying the attack upon the hero, he fell against the kitchen-table, upset the lamp, and very nearly set the house on fire.

Such a banging out of burning paraffin with mats, and throwing water about ensued as never was.

And when finally the conflagration was subdued the cook, instead of asking Cobb to proceed with his drama cut it short by boxing his ears.

Cobb thereupon went to bed in his little room on the roof, and spent a happy hour in softly practising on the concertina under the bedclothes.

He was getting up a few tunes which he calculated would charm 'Melia. But not having a very good ear he was unfortunately mixing them a bit.

"Nelly Bly" is a lively air, so is "Down by the River," likewise "The girl I left behind me;" but when delivered to the public in assorted bars they have a somewhat irritating effect upon the nerves.

However, Cobb that night escaped discovery, and, having got through his practice, sought repose, and found it.

On the morrow Jack was wonderfully better, but still very weak. He had, in a measure, recovered his voice, and it was deemed advisable for him to tell his story.

The inspector of police, Mr. Bangwell, and the doctor were present at the time.

"Tell the whole truth, Wyburn," said the schoolmaster.

"I am about to do so," replied Jack, "although the

beginning will, I am sure, excite your anger against me."

"I am willing to consider you have been sufficiently punished for any breach of discipline."

Jack appeared to be relieved by this declaration, and, entering upon his story, told them he had, in defiance of orders which he considered unjust, gone out of the house at a late hour.

"It was my intention," he said, "to have wandered about for awhile, nothing more, and then come back and have gone to bed."

"I went away by the back door, which had been locked up for the night, and I thought would pretty well sure to be open to me on my return.

"First I took a walk in the country," continued Jack, "returning to the town about half-past ten. I was in the mind to come in then, but there were lights in some of the upper windows, and I sauntered into the town for awhile. The High-street was empty, save for one person, who was sauntering ahead of me. I recognised in him a man named Sam Barlow."

"Steady, now," said the inspector, busy with his note-book. "You saw Sam Barlow coming towards you, I suppose?"

"No, going on ahead," returned Jack, "and walking briskly. I thought I would overtake him and have a chat, so I hurried up——"

"Steady—thought you would have a chat," said the inspector, jotting down the words, "so you went on, overtaking him?"

"No," said Jack, "he was too quick for me. He passed St. Peter's Church about twenty yards ahead of me, and I had just reached the gate when I suddenly lost consciousness. I fancy I was struck behind. The back part of my neck is very sore even now."

"Let me look at your neck," said the doctor, gently raising him. "H'm—yes—you were struck by something—a heavy shot encased in cloth, I should say. That would be a deadly weapon, and leave only the faintest mark behind it."

"About Sam Barlow, now," said the inspector. "You are sure you saw him?"

"Yes," said Jack.

"On ahead?"

"Certainly."

"And you did not overtake him?"

"No, not by about twenty yards, as I have already said."

"That settles it," said the inspector. "I've got the wrong man."

"Have you arrested Sam Barlow?" exclaimed Jack.

"Yes, I have," replied the inspector, looking rather foolish. "I thought he said enough to convict himself, but, of course, now it is all right. I'll set him free at once."

"Go on with your story, Wyburn," said Mr. Bangwell.

"I haven't much more to tell," said Jack. "When I came round I found myself lying in the dark, bound hand and foot, and I shouted for help until I was hoarse. I lost my voice, indeed, and never recovered it during the whole time I lay there suffering hunger and thirst. And sometimes I lost my senses, only to come back in a short time to my misery."

"And all the time you were lying there did you see or hear no one?" asked the doctor.

"The only sound I heard was the faint rumble of an occasional vehicle in the street, and the bells on the second night, when the ringers were practising," answered Jack.

"Well, inspector, what do you say to this?" asked Mr. Bangwell.

"Nothing, sir," the officer replied; "except that it leaves things in a state of *statu quo*. There's no evidence against anybody—to act upon."

"I feel sure that Mike Feeley had a hand in it," said Jack.

"That may be," exclaimed the inspector; "but your feeling sure would not convict him. However, you must leave the case in my hands, and I'll sift it, as far as I can, to the bottom."

He took his leave at once, very much vexed with himself, and half inclined to be angry with Sam Barlow for not being the guilty party.

Half-an-hour later Sam was a free man, on his way home to his wife, who was in a state of distraction on hearing of his incarceration.

His cottage was in one of the courts of the town, and, thanks to his drinking habits, it was very poorly furnished; but, to the credit of his wife, it was very clean.

Opening the door, he entered the front room, where a young and rather pretty woman was holding a little girl of four to her heart and crying bitterly.

"Sal!" he cried.

His wife uttered a scream of joy, and, springing up, threw herself upon his breast.

"Are you free, dear Sam?" she said.

"Free my lass," he said, "of two things—prison and the drink. I've got out of one, thanks to Master Wyburn, and the other I don't mean to be a slave of any more. A man as can't take a glass without making a brute of himself had better leave it alone, and that's what I'm about to do. Give us a kiss, old girl."

And Sal, without any mincing about the matter, after the manner of women, heartily complied.

CHAPTER XVIII.

COBB SEES NOT ONLY ONE GHOST BUT TWO.

BY the next day Jack had progressed so favourably that he was declared to be out of danger, and the restrictions on the boys to ensure quietude were removed.

This led to a reaction, and their animal spirits rose to an unaccustomed pitch, insomuch that a vent had to found, or something serious would happen.

I can't get along with these beastly lessons to-night," said Bob, closing his Lindley Murray.

"Do you ever get along with them?" asked Harry Farnborough, whom he addressed.

They were in the schoolroom with the other boys, getting up the lessons for the morrow, and the foregoing was an exchange of whispers.

"What can we do?" asked Bob.

"Suppose we go out and give Cobb or Biffins a scare?" suggested Harry. "One or the other of them is sure to be rung for directly."

"How?"

"Come out quietly, and I'll tell you."

Harry's plan was a very crude one. Simply to borrow two sheets from the beds, and, enveloping themselves in them, sit down in the hall until Cobb came. The charming simplicity of the thing ought to have ensured success, but it did so only in a qualified way.

The boys got themselves up and into position in about three minutes, and then placed a board on their knees bearing the words "Spectre Pupils." There they were in the hall waiting the ringing of the bell and the advent of Cobb or Biffins.

But it so happened that while they were getting the sheets upstairs Mr. Bangwell came down, and, meeting Cobb in the hall, forthwith led him into the schoolroom, to show him sundry corners from whence—when sweeping in the morning—he had failed to remove all the dirt, or, indeed, a fair portion of it.

Having given Cobb a short lecture in the presence of the boys—a lecture on sloth—he desired him to go back to the kitchen.

Cobb opened the door, caught sight of the two figures, and closed it again.

"Oh! lor," he gasped.

"What's the matter with you?" asked Mr. Bangwell, staring at his white face.

"Two ghostes," groaned Cobb.

"Where?"

"In the hall a sitting down."

Mr. Bangwell quietly took his cane from a corner behind the desk, and, followed by Cobb and some of the more curious of the boys, sallied out to lay the ghosts.

The unfortunate masqueraders could see the dim outline of sundry figures through the sheets, but could not distinguish who they were.

Thinking, however, it was only some of the boys, who were just as good material for a scare as Cobb or Biffins, they began to contort their bodies and groan in the orthodox sepulchral manner of authorised ghosts.

Bob was awakened to the real position of things by a cut of the cane that made him feel as if a red hot wire had been drawn across his thigh.

Springing up, he received another more to the rear—a third, and yet a fourth.

Terrified and smarting, he fell upon the floor, and with the assistance of other hands divested himself of his sheet.

Then he saw the grinning Cobb, a host of laughing boys, and the angry schoolmaster, cane in hand, glaring around him.

"There was another concerned in this outrage," said Mr. Bangwell. "Where is he?"

Harry had vanished, sheet and all, and nobody seemed to know what had become of him.

"Rudge, who was with you?" demanded Mr. Bangwell.

Bob, who had now got upon his feet, rubbed himself vigorously, but said nothing.

"Will you tell me who it was?"

"I'd rather not, sir."

"You will get double punishment if you do not."

"I'd rather have that, sir, than tell."

Mr Bangwell thereupon bestowed upon Bob a second castigation, which he bore with fortitude, being supported by the proud knowledge that he had in the presence of the whole school declined to peach.

Mr. Bangwell, having meted out vicarious punishment, informed Bob that an item for wilfully damaged bed linen would be put down in his bill, and departed.

"He can put down what he likes," said Bob. "What are you grinning at, Nutty?"

"You," replied Cobb; "you are a pretty sort to play a ghost."

"You were scared, anyway, Filberts," said Cecil Mead.

"I wasn't," said Cobb, loudly.

"Here, get away," said Cecil; "we don't want any of your cheek—go along with you!"

He gave Cobb a push, which sent him staggering a few steps. A terrible frown darkened his youthful brow.

"Beware of what you are doing of," he said, "or some dark deed may come of it."

"Will you go?" said Cecil, giving him another push.

Cobb lifted his shoulders to his ears, deepened his brow, and thrust his hand inside his jacket.

"Don't tempt me to do a des-es-prit deed," he threatened.

"Cobb wants cooling," said Tom Drake. "Let us carry him into the lavatory, and put his head under the tap."

Cobb beat a hasty retreat at once, growling awful threats. He knew that the boys were just as likely as not to carry out the suggestion.

The boys then went back to the schoolroom, where Bob, who was still engaged in rubbing the parts on which the heaviest blows had fallen, found Harry Farnborough calmly engaged with his books.

"You are a nice fellow!" cried Bob, "to sneak out of it like that."

"Now, I put it to you, said Harry, "what good would have come of my remaining?"

"You could have taken your share of the licking."

"And do you call that good?"

"I don't want to call it anything," said Bob. "I don't know that we need talk about it. The smart's all gone. But blow Bangwell, I say. When I'm a man I'll come over here especially to lick him."

Bob found great solace in this prospective vengeance, and having chuckled over it a bit, he resumed his studies and forgot his injuries.

They all said that he was a plucky fellow and deserved well of the whole school.

One boy, name Percy Thrower, of an enthusiastic disposition, went so far as to suggest that a subscription should be made for a testimonial to be presented to Bob in recognition of his meritorious refusal to split on a friend.

But this idea fell rather flat, pocket-money being just then very scarce, and Bob had to be contented with general approval.

Before going to rest, Cecil and Harry were permitted to visit Jack, who was lying in the spare bedchamber, an apartment reserved for guests.

They found him looking very cheerful, but far from his old self.

In reference to his incarceration in the church vault, he expressed a firm belief that both Mike Feeley and Buck Gruesum had a hand in it.

Mr. Bangwell quietly took his cane from
a corner behind the desk, and, followed
by Cobb and some of the more curious
of the boys, sallied out to lay the Ghosts.

"They owed me a grudge," he said, "and are just the men to settle it, if they could. But I think the balance is on my side now, *and I mean to pay it back*."

"Keep out of their way," said Cecil, "or they may murder you. I wonder they did not kill you outright as it is."

"I've an idea that they took a delight in my dying *slowly*," said Jack. "I've thought the matter over, and I feel sure that they came down one night to listen to my moans. I heard them, but at the time thought it was only the fancy of my semi-delirious condition."

"If you want any help to bring the beggars to grief," said Harry Farnborough, "you may rely on me."

"And me !" said Cecil.

"All right, dear boys," said Jack, gaily. "We'll talk over a plan when I get strong again."

He asked after Bob, and they told him about the ghost business, at which they laughed heartily.

"Poor old Bob !" he said. "Always in for it, if everybody else escapes."

"By-the-way, Jack," said Cecil, "have you been talking to any of the girls next door ?"

Jack looked at Cecil wonderingly.

"What on earth leads you to ask me such a question ?"

"But have you ?" pleaded Cecil.

"I've spoken to two or three," said Jack, carelessly ; "but only a word or so."

"You've not noticed anyone especially ?"

"No ! Why ?"

"Oh ! no reason in particular, Jack. I thought you might know. It's of no consequence."

It was on Jack's lips to reveal what he knew of Ned Goran's strange love-making, but he held his peace. After all, it was no affair of his.

When his chum left him he heard Cecil humming an air as he walked down the corridor.

"Something has made him happy," thought Jack. "I wonder why he asked that question ? I don't know that I want to be bothered with the girls."

Then he thought over the two or three he had smiled at or exchanged a word with, and presently there stood out from the rest a pretty face, with a wreath of hair of golden-brown about it, and he was thinking of that face when he fell asleep.

The tutors' room was, as we think we have mentioned before, just under the attic occupied by Cobb.

They had each a bed, and it was their habit to have a little conversation ere they sought repose.

Politics were at that late hour eschewed, and a less exciting topic was generally chosen for discussion.

On this particular evening they were talking of Miss Fillwell.

"A man might do worse than marry her," said Mr. Philpot.

"She's old, and somewhat scraggy," replied the other.

"My dear fellow, that woman has money, and a paying school. Her husband would practically be an independant man."

"Hush ! what is that ?" exclaimed Mr. Skaffer.

They both lay still, and then there fell upon their ears two short sharp groans, followed by a long, soul-harrowing wail.

"What *is* it ?" asked Mr. Philpot.

"Hush !" said the other.

The wail was repeated, and followed by half-a-dozen jumping squeaks.

"It's some animal on the roof," said Mr. Skaffer.

"Impossible !"

"It is—listen."

A strange series of sounds were now heard—spasmodic, sepulchral, and squeaky — a blood-chilling medley.

"Can't be cats," said Mr. Philpot.

"I don't know," replied Mr. Skaffer. "Cats are gifted with great vocal powers."

"I'll get up and scatter 'em," said Mr. Philpot, between his teeth.

He opened the window, and a most unearthly wail floated into the room.

"Hush !" said the tutor.

"Is that you, 'Melia ?" asked a voice, softly.

It was Cobb, who had been serenading his lady-love for the first time, he having, as he believed, succeeded in mastering the concertina.

Mr. Philpot did not recognise the voice, and a terrible fear took possession of him.

Closing the window quietly, he softly, cried—

"I say, Skaffer !"

"What is it ?" asked Mr. Skaffer, sleepily.

"There's burglars on the roof."

"Eh ?"

Mr. Skaffer was awake in a moment, and sitting up in the bed.

"Burglars," repeated Mr. Philpot. "I heard them talking."

CHAPTER XIX.

JACK RECEIVES ANOTHER LETTER—COBB IMPARTS SOME DISQUIETING INTELLIGENCE TO HIM.

 "WHAT'S to be done ?" exclaimed Mr. Philpot. "We ought to alarm Bangwell, of course. How many burglars are there ?" enquired Mr. Skaffer.

"I reckon three or four at least," said Mr. Philpot. "Yes, the safest course is to rouse Bangwell."

Mr. Philpot did not exactly like the job of rousing Mr. Bangwell, but, at the same time, he did not think he and his brother tutor should tackle the burglars alone.

So he went out of the room and knocked at the schoolmaster's door, which adjoined his own.

"Who's there ?" asked Mr. Bangwell.

"Get up, sir," replied Philpot ; "there's burglars on the roof of the house."

"Stuff ! It's cats."

"But I heard 'em talking."

"Nonsense ! It was somebody in the road. Go to bed again."

Mr. Philpot, feeling about the size of a three-penny-bit, went back to his room.

"He says it's cats," he said.

Mr. Skaffer, his brother tutor, who had meanwhile been under the bedclothes, emerged therefrom, and repeated, in quavery tones—"Cats ?"

"Yes ; and the voices came from somebody speaking in the road."

"Well, you may have been mistaken. There's the noise again !"

They were both quiet, and the sound, more mournful than anything they had yet heard, came from the outside.

It was no longer a musical instrument—Cobb was singing.

"Perhaps it's Persian cats," suggested Mr. Skaffer.

"Demon cats!" growled Mr. Philpot, as he again raised the window. "S-s-s-h! get away, you beasts, you—you—s-s-s-h!"

Then the noise ceased, and after a short period of unbroken silence the tutor, shivering, got into bed again.

"We must get some broken glass and put upon the tiles, Skaffer," he said; "also some poison and a trap. If that won't do I'll blow the beasts up with dynamite!"

.   .   .   .   .   .

"Here is a letter for you, Jack," said Cecil, on the fourth morning after Jack had been in the invalid's room.

He had so far recovered that he was out of bed and dressing when his friend appeared.

"A letter for *me?*" said Jack. "Rare things for me are letters. What does it look like?"

He remembered, with no very pleasant feeling, the anonymous letter he had received some time before, warning him against Gruesum.

"Look's like a girl's writing," said Cecil, "and is addressed 'Jack Wyburn, Esquire'—ahem! I saw it before Bangwell did, and thought it better to bring it along."

"It's scented, too," said Jack. "Now, who can it be from?"

He turned it over two or three times, and Cecil ventured to hint that the best way to get at the matter would be to open the envelope. "I am not curious," he added. "You needn't tell me anything about it unless you like."

"I can't fancy there being any reason to keep it a secret," said Jack.

He tore open the envelope and drew from the inside a folded sheet of grey-tinted paper. A wild flower, which had been enclosed in it, fell to the ground.

"Whew!" said Cecil, "that looks well."

Inside the sheet of paper was a few written words—

"*I am glad you are better.—F. M.*"

Nothing more.

"I don't know who 'F. M.' is," said Jack. "Here, Cecil, have a look at it. Can you help me?"

"Well," replied Cecil, after a glance at the letter, "I fancy it is somebody—who feels very kindly towards you."

The words did not come quite so freely as they might have done. Cecil remembered a pretty face, with a wreath of golden hair for a frame, which made a sweet picture of it, and a lump formed in his throat.

"Whoever she is," said Jack, "I thank her. It is kind, anyway."

He had not seen the flower fall, and turned away without attempting to pick it up.

Cecil stooped and secured it.

For a moment he seemed inclined to keep it, but honour forbade him to do so, and he resisted the impulse.

"Jack," he said, "here's a flower; it dropped out of the letter."

"Put it down," replied Jack, who had now prepared himself for a wash.

Cecil laid it on a table near, feeling rather glad that Jack seemed to care so little about it.

"By the way," said Jack, "have you seen anything of Sam Barlow?"

"Yes," said Cecil; "he's all right. They say he is likely to be made verger and head bellringer of the church. He's given up drink."

"What will Mike Feeley say to that?"

"It doesn't matter what he says. He's got the sack."

"Never!" exclaimed Jack, facing round, with the towel in his hands.

"Fact," said Cecil. "Although you couldn't swear that he and Gruesum attacked you, they have got the credit of it, and the vicar has sent Mike about his business."

"He is still in his house, of course?"

"No, he cleared out at once, and they tell me that he's gone down to a lonely cottage by the river."

"Well! that's news," said Jack. "Anything more?"

"A new boy is coming to-day. I heard Bangwell tell Philpot so."

"Know anything about him?"

"No—except that he is something special, for he is to have a room to himself."

"I wish him joy," said Jack; "he'll have a rough time of it here. We don't want any of the aristocracy to lord it over us."

"I should think not," said Cecil. "You seem wonderfully better, old man."

"I am," replied Jack. "I shall go out a bit this morning, and to-morrow I hope to be in the class-room again."

"We shall be glad to see you," said Cecil; "but if I were in your place I should make a month's holiday over this business."

"No, you wouldn't."

"Dan would."

"Oh! he's a horse of another colour."

The breakfast-bell at that moment rang, and Cecil hastened out of the room. Jack finished his dressing and went slowly downstairs.

It was a beautiful fresh morning, and he thought he would go into the open air for a few moments. A saunter in the back garden would do him good.

On his way he had to pass the dining-room, from whence came the sounds of clattering mugs and plates and the faint buzz of voices.

"To think how near I've been to never hearing their voices again!" thought Jack, with a shudder. "Horrible!"

It was an unusual thing for pupils to go into the back garden, it being reserved by the schoolmaster for his own use; but Jack had been desired to make use of it when he could get abroad.

Everybody was kind to him just then, and none more so than Mr. and Mrs. Bangwell, but Jack did not want any coddling.

It was his intention to resume his old life as soon as possible.

Cobb was just outside the back door, engaged in packing some empty beer bottles in a box.

"Good morning, Master Wyburn," he said, approvingly. "Glad to see you out again."

"Thank you," replied Jack. "I am very much better."

" I suppose," said Cobb, lowering his voice, " that you ain't got the perpetrators of the deed within thy grasp?"

"No," said Jack.

"But dost thou know who it is?" asked Cobb, drawing his head back and frowning heavily.

" I can guess, of course," said Jack; "but that's no use."

"Hast thou no evidence?"

"None good enough."

"Ah!" said Cobb, folding his arms and pursing his lips, "there is an 'alo of mystery about the job, but it will be cleared away and the sword of justice come down on the offenders like a heavylanch. I might say something, but no—not yet."

"Cobb," said Jack, "if you know anything, out with it. If you don't, drop the stage business."

"It ain't stage," said Cobb, "it's real life. I've got a clue."

"Well, what is it?" asked Jack, rather impatiently.

"Has thou ever in thy wanderings offended one Ned Goran?" asked Cobb.

" I am afraid I have," replied Jack.

"And another whose name is Chicks? Is there not ill-blood between thee?"

"A little—on his part."

"H'm! ha! so," said Cobb. "I com-pre-hend!"

"Look here, Cobb," said Jack, "you've got to speak out, or I shall be knocking your head against the wall."

"May I speak out my own way?" asked Cobb.

"Yes."

"If I put it in a drammyatic form you won't cut me short?"

"No."

"Then, listen," said Cobb, folding his arms; "but first close yon door. Thanks. The prying Biffins may be abroad. On the night when thou, Friend Wyburn, went forth in defiance of the tyrant's fryat—"

"The what?" asked Jack.

"Fryat—order, command," replied Cobb.

"Oh! fiat," said Jack. "Go on."

"On that night, at a certain hour, two knaves were in council within the shadow of the front porch of this lordly mansion.

"'I hate him!' saith one.

"'He's poison to me,' saith the other.

"'I'd like to knock his head orf,' saith the previc party.

"'And I'll help you to do it, and bury him, needs be.'

"Then they walked into the house and journeyed upstairs, and it was my intention to have follered and listened more, when missus rung for coals, and I was foiled."

Despite the fantastic way Cobb narrated the above, Jack saw that it was worthy of serious attention.

"You know who these two were?" he said.

"I do," answered Cobb; "first their voices, and then their forms, I recognised."

"And their names?"

"Let me softly whisper them in thine ear."

Jack bent down, and Cobb, shielding his mouth with his hand, whispered just loud enough to be heard—

"Goran and Chicks."

"Now Cobb," said Jack, "I must tell you that this is a very serious thing."

"It's the truth," replied Cobb; "if I'm biled in oil, and afterwards sent to the stake for it."

"It gives me a very different view to that I've entertained of the attack upon me," said Jack; "but at the same time it is only hearsay. Were they out of the house that night?"

"I cannot say," replied Cobb. "Perchance they were, as they have been afore."

"Are you sure of that?"

"I've seen 'em go and come back again. I've met 'em out, and Biffins knows it, too."

"How is it he hasn't reported them?"

"Because he goes out hisself," said Cobb. "Only now and then I has a hour sometimes."

"But what do you get up to, Cobb?" asked Jack.

"Nothing to be ashamed of," said Cobb. "I likes to get into some lonely part of the town and play at waiting for my prey. I fancies myself a robber chief. It's thrilling, but too lonely. I often wish I had one of my men with me; but as yet I haven't got any men."

"You had better keep at home," said Jack. "One of these nights you will get into trouble."

"At present," said Cobb, "I have given up the robber business, and am a playing of the trouble-door on the tiles; but, somehow, Melia don't seem to grasp the sitivation yet."

"You will get found out at that."

"I've been heard by them tutors," said Cobb, chuckling; "luckily they have got no ear for music, and cuss me for cats. I say, Mister Wyburn, I don't want to be drawed into a row with anybody. If you tells them partner villains—"

"I won't say anything," said Jack. "But you have given me a clue, and I will see what I can work out of it."

Cobb laid his finger on his lip and frowned, to indicate that the utmost secrecy was indeed important, and then, having put the bottles in order, disappeared.

.   .   .   .   .   .

After breakfast and a short rest, Jack left the school and sauntered into the town. He had previously acquainted Mr. Bangwell with his desire to do so, and received his sanction.

"But do not go too far," was the schoolmaster's injunction, "for you are still very weak—and be sure you do not go out of the main thoroughfare."

Jack had no apprehension of an attack being made upon him in the daylight, and he had no intention of going far away.

It was very sweet to be in the open air after several days' confinement to a sick-room, for even sluggish Moatborough was comparatively gay to it.

A very short walk brought him to St. Peter's Churchyard, and glancing through the iron gates, he saw that the door of the belfry was open.

Remembering that Mike Feeley had been discharged, he naturally supposed that it was Sam Barlow who was in the church, and sauntered into the belfry to have a chat with him.

Sam was not there, nor anybody else—nor was there anyone within the main body of the church.

Jack was about to saunter out again, when his eyes fell upon the entrance to the flight of steps leading to the bell-chamber above.

"Perhaps Sam is up there," he thought. "He won't mind my going up to him."

A little curiosity to know what a bell-chamber

was like had something to do with his desire. He had never been in one in his life.

So he went up the narrow-winding way to the resting-place of the bells.

It was empty—like the church below, and he turned to the bells to examine how they were fixed, an occupation that gave him several minutes of interest. He was aroused from it by a footstep on the stairs.

Somebody was coming up in a sneaking yet lumbering way—a heavy-footed, cautious way of advancing.

A sudden feeling akin for a moment to fear overcame him.

Recent suffering and illness had naturally weakened him. He was far from being himself, but the momentary agitation passed away and he was ready to meet anybody.

Up, came that heavy footfall—slowly, step by step, until the head of Buck Gruesum appeared.

What Jack apprehended had come true. It was the ruffian following him—for mischief perhaps.

"I want a word with you," said Gruesum, as he stepped into the bell-chamber. "I saw you come into the church and I followed in on purpose."

"I would rather not have a word with you, as you call it," answered Jack.

"But you've got to have it whether you like it or not," said Gruesum.

He carried a heavy stick in his hand, as he usually did, but he did not as yet make any demonstration with it.

His manner was rather inclined to be roughly persuasive than aggressive.

"I wish you to know," said Gruesum, "that I've got a character, and it's not to be took away."

"I should have thought," replied Jack, "that you would be very glad to get rid of it."

"What d'ye mean by that?"

"It is a character few men would care to keep."

"You gents," said Gruesum, "ha' got a quiet, snarling way of speaking to a poor man, but it won't do for me. I tell you *not* to take my character away, whatsomever it may be."

"How have I done so?"

"You put that 'ere job on me."

"What job?"

"Don't you mock me," cried Gruesum, raising his stick with a threatening air. "You know very well what I mean."

Jack never budged a hair, but looked him straight in the face, unflinchingly.

"You're a low bully," he said; "a blackguard, and capable of anything."

"I warn you not to say too much to me," hissed Gruesum. "I could settle you in about five seconds."

"But you dare not," returned Jack, coolly.

"Daren't I?"

"No; you are sure to have been seen by somebody coming in, and very likely will be seen by others as you go out. If I should be found murdered here they would know whom to charge with it."

Under the coarse red of the ruffian's countenance there was a leaden hue—the hue of impotent fury.

"The bare thought of hanging," continued Jack, "makes you pause. Again, I say you dare not kill me, nor even strike me."

"What, ain't you done yet? I—"

Gruesum paused his voice dying away into a whisper; the sound of footsteps below had reached him. Jack heard them too, also the voices of the vicar and Sam Barlow.

Jack knew he was saved then, and in the joy of the moment could have rushed downstairs.

But he kept cool, and walking slowly across the bell-chamber, said—

"Gruesum, you have just given me a warning. Let me give you one in return. If you ever dare to speak to me again I'll never leave you until I see you safely lodged in prison."

Gruesum did not answer him, but stood dumb with fury against the woodwork of one of the frames supporting the bells.

But for his being a coward in heart he would have committed murder then.

Jack, knowing he had something of a wild beast to deal with, backed down the first few stairs, keeping his eye upon the ruffian while he was in sight.

On reaching the belfry he found the vicar and Sam Barlow examining one of the ropes which had the appearance of being cut half through.

"It has been done by somebody," Sam was saying, "and whoever it was has got a duplicate key of the belfry."

"We must have the place watched," replied the vicar. Then, catching sight of Jack, he exclaimed, "Bless me! you here?"

"I came out for a stroll, sir," replied Jack, as he took the vicar's proffered hand, "and, seeing the belfry open, came in, hoping to find Barlow."

He gave Sam his hand, which Sam, after he had given his own a rub on his corduroy trousers, accepted.

"I hope I have not done wrong in going above," Jack continued. "I have not been there alone."

"If there are any other boys up there," said the vicar, "they ought to come down."

"There is only one—a man," rejoined Jack; "a man."

"Who is he?" asked Sam Barlow.

"That ruffian Gruesum," replied Jack. "He followed me up to try his hand at bullying me. He says I've taken his character away, and he won't stand it."

"Buck Gruesum," said Sam Barlow, "ain't got any right up there. I'll just fetch him down."

It was on the vicar's tongue to ask him to have no brawling in the church; but ere he could utter the words Sam, in a heated state, had started upstairs. A short way up he came upon Gruesum, who was coming down.

The narrowness of the staircase has been already mentioned. There was no possibility of the men fairly meeting. Sam's head came against Gruesum's knees.

"Come out here!" said Sam, unceremoniously, as he grasped the other by the ankles.

A backward step or two, with corresponding jerks, landed Gruesum in the belfry on his back.

"Barlow—Barlow!" cried the vicar; "no violence."

"There's been no violence, sir," answered Sam, "but he's not the man to use soft soap."

"The best thing to be done with him," said the vicar, deliberately, "is to lock him up. There is an officer outside. Call him in."

"Don't do that," said Gruesum, with a threaten-ing air, " or you may be sorry for it."

He was getting upon his feet, but Sam pushed him down again, and Jack went outside for a policeman, performing the task with a feeling of intense satisfaction.

Buck Gruesum made no resistance.

The officer came in, and being told that the ruffian was to be charged with loitering in the church under suspicious circumstances, just took him by the arm above the elbow.

"You come along," he said.

Gruesum hung his head, and after one malevo-lent glance at the vicar was led away.

We may as well at once announce that, on being taken before the magistrates, and duly charged with being in the church under suspicious circumstances, the bench, glad of an opportunity of " giving him something," sent him to prison for a month.

CHAPTER XX.

THE NEWCOMER—BEN CHICKS PLAYS HIS OLD ROLE OF BULLY—NERVOUS, BUT NOT A COWARD.

JACK was away so long that when he returned to the school the morning studies were over, and the boys were in the playground. As he entered the gate he was espied by several of his chums, who came running towards him.

"Glad to see you, old fellow !"

"Do you feel strong again ?"

"You look almost as well as ever !"

In this style they greeted him, and the congratu-lations were almost general.

Ben Chicks and his limited following held aloof.

Jack told them that Gruesum was locked up, a piece of news hailed with excitement and delight, and then Bob Rudge gave him a piece of intelli-gence.

"The new boy's come," he said.

"What is he like ?" asked Jack.

"Haven't seen him—none of us ; but we've had a peep at his boxes—regular swell things."

"He is a swell," said Harry Farnborough, "or he wouldn't have a private room, and he seems to stick to it. He's there now."

"Don't fib," said Tom Drake. "Here he is, coming out."

A good-looking, tall lad of fifteen was coming out of the house in a quiet way, as if he did not wish to be seen.

He cast a half-shy look around him and walked slowly in the direction of the comparatively-deserted part of the playground.

"Hang it all !" said Jack. "Somebody ought to speak to him."

"There goes Chicks," said Harry ; "he means to do the civil."

"No, he doesn't," replied Jack. "Look at the leer on his face. He means to chaff the fellow. That isn't right. He's a stranger, and until we know he is *not* a good fellow we ought to treat him as one."

He hurried towards the lad, but Chicks was there before him, and he put himself right in the way of the stranger, bowing almost to the ground.

"Welcome, my lord," he said, "to our humble rookery."

The newcomer stopped short, and with a flushed face looked quickly about him, not exactly in a frightened way, but it was a very peculiar look.

"Who do you mean by ' my lord ?' " he asked.

"Are you not a lord ?" inquired Chicks, in mock surprise.

The newcomer was now composed. He looked at Chicks with speaking eyes, bright with restrained anger, but he said not a word.

CHAPTER XXI.

STRAIGHT FROM THE SHOULDER.

"THAT will do, Chicks," said Jack, as he came up. "You need not make a fool of yourself."

"Oh ! of course you must interfere," sneered Chicks.

"It isn't right to insult a new fellow," said Jack. "You may think it funny, but nobody else does. Welcome to Bangwell School," he said to the stranger.

"Thank you," was the quiet reply.

"The usual thing," continued Jack, "is to let us know who you are."

"He's Lord Standoff !" sneered Chicks.

"Why don't you be quiet, Chicks ?" said Harry Farnborough. "What an ass you are !"

"I'll trouble *you* to be civil," replied Chicks.

"I am sorry," interposed the newcomer, "that there should be any bother on my account. What do you want to know ? My name, of course."

"If you wish to give it," returned Jack.

"Certainly—Harold Gillispie is my name. I am of a fairly respectable family, considered to be rich by some people, and it is my humour to be left as much as possible to myself. I mean no offence."

"You can be left entirely to yourself if you wish it," retorted Chicks.

"His tongue goes like a mill wheel," said Bob Rudge. "Clicketty clack—clicketty clack. Don't mind him, Gillispie."

"I don't mind him," replied Gillispie ; "but I don't like every dog to bark at me."

"Do you call me a dog ?" fiercely demanded Ben.

"I think you behave very much like one," was the quiet reply.

Ben strode up to the speaker. He did not budge.

"What a shame !" muttered Harry Farnborough ; " pitching on a fellow the first day he is here."

"Let him alone," said Jack. "I fancy he can take care of himself. He seems to me to be natur-ally nervous, but he is not a coward."

"You say again that I am a dog," growled Chicks.

"I never said 'it at all," answered Gillispie. "I merely said you behaved like one."

"Well ! say that again."

"Oh ! bosh. I can't be bothered in this way. What do you want ?"

"An apology," said Chicks.

"Then you certainly won't get it," was the answer. "Don't let us have any brawling. I only want to be let alone."

"But you've insulted me vilely," said Chicks, " and I WILL have an apology."

Harold Gillispie faintly smiled, and moved aside as if to walk away.

Chicks seized him by the collar.

"You stop here," he hissed, "and apologise."

The next moment he lay at full length upon the ground, blinking and spluttering, and the stream of life flowing freely from his nose.

Gillispie had knocked him down, and the thing was so quickly done that half the boys did not see it.

But those who did afterwards said they had never seen so quick a blow, or one straighter from the shoulder.

"That is my apology to you," said Gillispie, and walked away.

They let him go, and two or three of the chosen chums of Chicks picked him up from the ground.

One of them, named Railton, observed—

"You had better pop your handkerchief to your nose, or your clothes will be in a fearful mess."

Chicks mechanically drew his handkerchief from his pocket and placed it to his nose. In a wild-eyed, terrified way, he looked about him.

"I've had enough," he mumbled. "I give in—don't hit me any more, please."

"Bah!" exclaimed Harry Farnborough. "And to think that some of us have been afraid of him. Come away, Jack."

Whatever Harold Gillispie may have thought of his easy victory over Chicks he showed no outward sign of having done anything out of the common.

He sauntered about by himself until the dinner-bell, vigorously rung by Biffins, as if he wished it to be heard a mile away, summoned the boys to dinner.

Then he went in with the rest, ate his dinner in silence, and afterwards stole away to his private room. Nothing more was seen of him until studies were renewed, and then he took a seat near Mr. Bangwell's desk, allotted to him by the school-master, and gave himself up to his books.

After that the boys saw him no more until supper-time, which he partook of in the same silent way.

As he was leaving the room he said, "Good-night, gentlemen," and a few responded, but the majority said nothing, and more than one grinned.

Chicks—who had two promising black eyes in the course of development, and had not been asked by Mr. Bangwell or the ushers from whence he got them, which was a little unusual—had a sneer for the new comer, after he was gone.

"He's the son of a prize-fighter," he said.

"Don't you wish you were?" innocently asked Bob Rudge, and all who heard it, to Ben's mighty wrath, laughed.

Jack, by his own desire, returned that night to his old bed in the dormitory, and as the boys were undressing they discussed Harold Gillispie.

"I don't understand him at all," said Cecil Mead, "but somehow I begin to like him."

"That 'Good-night, gentlemen,' fetched me," said Bob Rudge, "and did you notice how he said it. As natural as if he were a man talking to a lot of youngsters. Hullo! who's been splitting open the collar of my night-shirt. No, it's all right; I've got it upside down. 'Good-night, gentlemen.' Good Heavens! what next?"

There was some laughing over what Bob said, but it was admitted all round that Harold Gillispie was a bit strange. "A novelty in schoolboys," Harry Farnborough called him.

"His quiet, reserved ways are nothing," said Jack. "I'll be bound he is a good fellow."

"May be," said Harry, with a yawn; "but what is the good of his being a good fellow if he doesn't mix with us?"

"Perhaps he will one day," said Jack. "I fancy he is under a cloud."

"What sort of cloud?" asked Bob. "Dash it! somebody's made me a bread and butter bed. I tell you fellows that if—"

"Here he comes," said Cecil Mead.

A rush was made for the beds. Jack blew out the light, and there was much feigning of sleeep when Mr. Philpot opened the door and looked in.

He counted the heads and retired.

Then Bob uncurled himself, and in the dark proceeded to right his bread and butter bed, which, as most people know, is the under sheet folded upwards so as to make a stretch down impossible.

"I'll bet you did it, Harry," said Bob. "Why can't you let things alone? Dash it! I shall never get it right. How would you like it? Crumbs! what a mixture of blanket and sheet I've got here. I must roll myself up in it somehow. Are you all asleep?"

No answer.

"Good-night, gentlemen," said Bob, in imitation of Harold Gillispie.

A general laugh followed.

"I thought you couldn't be asleep," muttered Bob. "Goodness! what a bed. It's like sleeping on a heap of rags. I can see the item 'extra bed linen' down in the bill. Harry, you are a beast!"

CHAPTER XXII.

THE STRANGE NEW BOY—A PUZZLING STATE OF THINGS—A PAINFUL DISCOVERY.

ACK WYBURN was not the sort of boy to thrust himself upon anyone who did not want him. Nevertheless, in spite of the coldness of Harold Gillispie, he could not help seeking his society.

The newcomer, however, held aloof, and quietly repelled all advances.

There was nothing offensive in his way of doing so. On the contrary, it was done in a very pleasant manner. But the fact remained—he neither sought others nor desired them to seek him.

Bob Rudge was rather indignant about it.

"He's a stuck-up ass," he said, "and ought to be sent to Coventry."

"Rather a needless thing to do," replied Harry Farnborough, "seeing that he has chosen to go there of his own accord."

Naturally such a strange youth would excite the attention of the whole house, and everybody formed an opinion of him. Cobb's notion of the cause of his reserve was characteristic.

"He's done something," he said to Biffins, as the

pair were engaged in the pantry knife and plate cleaning.

"Who ?" asked Biffins.

"That new boy."

"When did he do it ?"

"I don't know," replied Cobb ; "but it's something serious—a big robbery, or a murder."

'Get out !" said Biffin, turning ghastly pale.

'I tell you it is so," said Cobb, firmly. "I ain't read books for nothing. He's got a murderer's eye —quiet and de-ter-mined. He's got a habit, too, of putting his hand to his waist, jest as if he'd been used to carrying of a dagger in his girdle."

"Good 'evens !" exclaimed Biffins. "Only to think of it !"

Biffins for some time past had looked very pale. He had spoken of feeling unwell, and the cook made up for him a certain medicine—her mother's own prescription—for his benefit.

It consisted of several very active chemicals, and a full-sized dose would have been a serious thing for a horse to take ; but it had no effect on Biffins.

"I ain't no better," he told the cook. "It's a sort of all-over 'eaviness I've got. Generally done up, I am."

After the dread insinuations of Cobb he became worse, and went about in such a limp condition that it was pitiful to see him.

All round there was a tendency to derangement in the school.

Vague rumours of Mr. Bangwell having himself seen a ghost got about, and after dark nobody cared to go about the old house alone.

Mysterious tappings were heard on the walls, although the precise spot could not be located. Other minor matters helped to raise a ferment, and the climax came one night, when the alarm-bell rang again.

Not only did it ring louder than ever, but it was followed by a cry of "Murder !" and sounds of a desperate scuffle were heard in the hall.

It was brief, but it alarmed the whole house, and Mr. Bangwell and the tutors, each armed with a poker, stole softly down, keeping in a line on the broad staircase, as none of them seemed anxious to assume the place of leader.

But all they found was an overturned chair, and the boots of the boys, generally in rows for Cobb to take away and clean, scattered about in every direction.

On visiting Biffins' room they found Biffins asleep and snoring, with an empty jug on a chair by his bedside.

That jug smelt strongly of beer, and his heavy condition of sleep was accounted for.

"The drunken scoundrel !" said Mr. Bangwell. "I'll discharge him in the morning."

On examining the doors of the house they found the scullery one unbolted.

"This is the way they got in," said Mr. Philpot.

"And went out again," sagaciously added Mr. Skaffer.

"But who are they ?" asked Mr. Bangwell. "Why should outside people come here to ring my alarm bell, cry murder, and disarrange everything in the hall ?"

"That's a poser," replied Mr. Philpot.

So it was, and a poser it remained for that night at least.

Having gone over the whole place, including the cellar, wherein the cat of the house, scratching among the coals, gave them all a fit of the jumps, the three gentlemen returned upstairs to quiet the rest of the inmates with the vague assurance that "it was nothing."

It was quite an hour, however, ere the majority of the occupants could get to sleep again.

On Jack Wyburn there was a strange watchfulness, which he could not overcome.

It was not that he felt alarmed or anything approaching it, nor even dread or anxiety. It was simply wakefulness, and nothing more.

One by one he heard the breathing of his chums settle down into the long stride of sleep, and then came the almost complete stillness which rests upon a house in the country in the middle of the night.

And it seemed to him that his hearing had suddenly become very acute.

He fancied he could hear the soft footfall of a cat in the corridor outside, and the infinitesimal scratching footfall of a wandering beetle ; but these things were clearly fancy.

But presently he heard a sound which was tolerably clear. It was like the click of a latch below.

Lying motionless, he soon heard it again followed by the subdued rattling which accompanies the trying of a fastened, but loosely-fitting door.

If no other feeling but curiosity prompted him, it sufficed for him to get out of bed, open the door of the dormitory, and listen.

But although he strained his ears, and stood at his post for some time, he did not hear it again.

"I could not have imagined it," he muttered, as he got again between the sheets.

Barely had he settled down into watchful stillness when he heard it once more.

Undoubtedly it was the click of a latch, and somebody trying a door.

It was at the back of the house, too, he felt sure.

The window of the dormitory looked out on the playground in front, and he had no opportunity of seeing who it was. All he could do was to lie still and await developments.

And nothing developed.

The sounds were not heard again.

But Jack slept no more that night.

He did everything he could to lure sleep to his eyelids, but the drowsy god refused to come, and the morning found him weary, pale, and pretty well worn out with his enforced watchfulness.

The boys all noticed it, and Harry Farnborough asked him if he had taken cold.

"No," he said. "I have been rather wakeful in the night, nothing more."

But if Jack looked pale the boys were soon to see one looking much worse.

As they were descending the stairs they found Harold Gillispie coming up.

He was not walking but crawling, and dragging one leg painfully after the other. His face was ghastly white.

Without taking any notice of them he went by, and they said nothing until he had disappeared

"What does he look like ?" said Cecil Mead, drawing a deep breath.

"As if he had been out all night," replied Harry.

"There is something very odd about the fellow and his ways," said Jack ; "but we won't be in a hurry to judge him. You know it is not *our* affair."

THE
BANGWELL BOYS
BEING THE SEQUEL TO
Hardiboy James ; or, Chums and Chappies.

Gillispie's body quivered with emotion, but he made no reply.

They agreed that it was not, and Jack's view of the matter was pretty well confirmed an hour later by Cobb, who requested "the honour of a private interview."

His request was granted, and, in the seclusion of the pantry, Cobb imparted a dread secret to Jack.

"When I opened the back door this morning," he said, "Master Gillispie was waiting to come in."

"Waiting—where?" exclaimed Jack.

"Jest outside, on the step. He looked almost dead, but he said nothing, except 'Thank you,' as he walked in with a tottering footstep."

"Cobb!" said Jack, "you must say nothing about this until I give leave to you to do so."

"Bind me on my oath," said Cobb, "or I'm afraid I sha'n't keep it."

"You have not said anything about it to anybody, I hope?"

"No, Master Wyburn, I ain't. I don't want to be had up for an accessory after the fact."

"What fact?"

"Highway robbery or murder—in course he's been up to one or the other."

"Nonsense—stuff," said Jack. "Your mind, Cobb, is always running on these things. It's not so bad as that, whatever it is. Remember, I ask you to say nothing."

Cobb strode out with a handful of knives from one tray and half a dozen forks from another.

Holding these aloft, he said, in a fervent tone—

"I swear!"

CHAPTER XXIII.

A PERILOUS LOVE ADVENTURE—COBB CHANGES HIS VIEWS ABOUT THE JOYS OF COURTSHIP.

E have now briefly to record the sudden termination of a wooing.

Owing to the strange rumours about the house, Cobb no longer dare venture to serenade his lady-love 'Melia on the tiles; but being of a persevering nature he decided to vocally charm her as the sun rose, and, for that purpose, one morning stepped out of the window of his room in the roof, concertina in hand.

There had been a dew on the previous evening, followed by a midnight frost, so that the tiles were slippery.

Cobb slipped.

In one brief moment, occupied in sliding down the tiles, all the possibilities following a fall into the playground flashed upon him.

He saw himself a mangled corpse, his being picked up dead, heard the wail of his parents, and was just entering on the scene of an inquest being held upon him, when he came to a dead stop.

He had got over the leaden gutter, and in the act of his falling had been caught by one of the hooks supporting it.

It was a strong hook, and, having got under his jacket, it held him.

Throughout his brief but dreadful flight Cobb held on to his concertina.

He could the more easily do this because one of his hands was fixed in the strap attached for that purpose.

What an awful position he was in!

If he should lose his jacket-hold upon the hook, down he would go—and then? Ugh!

But what was he to do?

He could not serenade 'Melia now—indeed, all thoughts of that fascinating young person had gone out of his head.

Cobb concentrated his thoughts on his own personal safety.

What should he do? Should he shout for help?

That was as good a thing as he could have done under certain circumstances; but he felt he could not do it without danger. A shout might bring him down.

Should he wait until everybody was up? Then he would have a very good chance of being seen and rescued.

That was all very well; but it would be at least an hour before the boys came into the playground, and passers-by in the road, from whence he could be seen, were very scarce at that time in the morning.

Then he thought of his concertina.

Happy thought!

With great care, so as to avoid any dangerous action, he drew it out and closed it again, with his fingers on the lower keys.

The result was something like a dismal groan.

Then he placed his digits on the upper notes, and brought forth a kind of shriek.

"Will anybody hear it?" he asked himself.

Now it so happened that Mr. Philpot, bent on taking an early morning walk, was at that time engaged in dressing.

He heard the sounds, and, addressing his fellow usher wrapped up in the bedclothes, said—

"Here are those blessed cats again!"

"What did you say?" sleepily asked Mr. Skaffer

"The cats again," said Mr. Philpot.

"Oh! hang 'em," growled Mr. Skaffer, covering up his ears.

"I will if I can get hold of them," muttered Mr. Philpot.

Again a dismal wail was heard, and Mr Philpot, angrily raising the window, thrust half his body out.

The sight of a boy, apparently suspended in the air, playing a concertina, fairly took his breath away. Not recognising Cobb on the instant, thoughts of cherubs rose in his mind, to be speedily dispelled by the unfortunate one.

"Oh! sir, I'm hung up here. Please help me down!"

"Cobb!" exclaimed Mr. Philpot, on recognising him. "What are you doing there?"

"Please, sir, I'm hooked up, and if I ain't soon taken down I shall fall a buster and be killed. The stitches are a giving."

Well, to make this part of the story short, an alarm was raised, and in a few minutes a dozen people, including Mr. Bangwell and some of the boys, were outside looking up at the aërial Cobb.

They got a blanket, and held it out in case he

should fall, while Biffins, who was in a state of wild excitement, was sent to the yard of a builder to borrow a ladder.

First of all he brought one much too short, and Cobb, all the time shrieking that the stitches were giving, was in peril each moment of falling.

The next ladder brought was still short; but it served, and a sturdy workman, who helped Biffins to bring it, ascended to release the hapless youth, and bring him down.

"Now, don't you wriggle, nor do nothing," he said to Cobb, "but just trust to me. Drop that ere concertina."

Cobb did so, and Mr. Skaffer, who was busy underneath re-arranging the blanket in case of a fall, received it on his head.

The note it gave then was the last it ever uttered, for the usher, led away by momentary wrath, put his foot through it on the ground, and crushed out its musical existence. Cobb was got down without mishap, but the strain upon his mental resources had been very great, and he was practically speechless when he arrived below.

He was assisted into the house by Biffins, and led into the kitchen, where he was put into a chair to recover himself.

When he did come round he was exceedingly reticent about the real facts of the case.

He was not quite sure how it had all come about.

"I suppose," he said, "I must have walked there in my sleep."

"Bosh!" said Biffins. "Nobody ever walks in their sleep. What do you mean by humbugging me?"

Then Biffins boxed his ears, so did the cook, and afterwards he had an interview with Mr. Bangwell, in that gentleman's private room, from which he emerged in a flushed and most miserable condition.

"And all on account of a measly sort of gal," said Cobb, as he gathered up the boots to be cleaned. "No more courting for me—it don't pay. I'll live and die a bacheldoor."

CHAPTER XXIV.

A MEETING IN A GREEN LANE—CECIL MEAD IS TROUBLED—BOB RUDGE DOES A BIT OF RABBITTING.

HALF holiday had come round again, and, the day being fine, the boys were all abroad.

Jack Wyburn and Cecil Mead went out together for a stroll, the former not feeling quite fit for a run across country in a game of "hare and hounds."

A sense of sadness was on Jack, for under his usual brave and merry bearing there lay an element of poetry—a good thing under control, but when in the possession of a weak nature it is apt to degenerate into a maudlin spirit. There was no fear, however, of it doing so in Jack's case, but he had the feeling stirring within him.

It had been roused by another anonymous letter, expressing pleasure on seeing that he was getting quite well after the recent "dastardly attempt upon his life."

"I can't think who has written those letters," he said to Cecil, as they strolled into a quiet lane about a mile from Moatborough. "What do you think of them?"

"It is one of Miss Fillwell's girls writing to you," replied Cecil, with a lump in his throat.

He had a shrewd suspicion who the author was, but, with all his loyalty to Jack, it was not in his power to be more explicit.

"I want *not* to think of her," he said to himself, "but it is no good."

Then he was angry with himself, and, like most boys of his age, felt ashamed that any girl should have the power of giving him the least uneasiness.

"I'll tell him to-morrow," he murmured, "and then he can do as he pleases. Perhaps he won't care for her."

The boys strolled on, Jack falling into a day dream, from which he was aroused by Cecil laying a hand upon his arm.

"Hush!" he whispered; "there are two people talking on the other side of the fence, and one is Ned Goran."

"I don't want to listen," r plied Jack.

But he was compelled t listen a little bit, for the passionate voice of a girl was heard asking Ned Goran to leave her.

"Why do you follow and persecute me?" she asked. "Have I not told you that I dislike you?"

"I will *make* you like me," answered Ned Goran.

There was no mistaking his voice, although he was undoubtedly agitated.

"I thought I was safe for one day," continued the girl. "I have been to visit a relative, and nobody but Miss Fillwell and myself knew I was going."

"I am watching for you day and night," said Ned Goran. "I can't help it. Oh! if you—"

"Let go of me! How dare you!"

"I can't. I love you."

"Here," said Jack, "this won't do. He's insulting the girl."

"You are no match for him. He is much older than you," said Cecil, hurriedly.

"I will see if it is so," said Jack.

He sprang up the bank, forced his way through the hedge, and found himself in view of a scene that set his blood tingling.

A girl was struggling in the grasp of Ned Goran, who was endeavouring to kiss her.

It was quickly done. A blow, and Ned Goran was down. The girl clasped Jack's arm, uttering a cry of delight.

"Don't be alarmed," said Jack. "I will take care of you."

Cecil Mead now came slowly through the opening Jack had made in the hedge, and took all in at a glance.

"Oh! if it had but been *me*, instead of Jack," he thought.

But it was not him, and there was an end of it. Loyally he went to the support of his friend and unconscious rival.

"You are not fit to fight, Jack," he said. "If Goran shows his teeth I will tackle him."

"Nothing of the sort," replied Jack. "You look after this lady. Now don't be alarmed, if you please. I don't think there will be much violence."

"He is not fit to fight—not strong enough," said Miss Whymper. who proved to be the young lady insulted, to Cecil. "Do not let him do it."

"There will be no fight," replid Cecil, briefly.

Ned Goran was now rising from the ground, with a thin streak of blood running from the corner of his lip down his chin.

Never before had Jack seen him so malevolent.

But he was very quiet.

"This is a planned thing between you, I reckon," he said. "But I'll square accounts with you both."

"Get away, you miserable hound," said Jack. "What do you mean by a planned thing? I do not even know this young lady."

"Hasn't she been writing to you?" hissed Ned Goran. "You can't deny it. *I've seen the letter.* If you *don't* know her, what sort of a girl is she to write to you, I ask?"

"Knock him down again, Jack," cried Cecil.

But ere the words had left his lips it was done.

Jack, indignant at the taunt thrown at the girl, and a pretty one to boot, went for Goran and knocked him over.

The resistance made was very feeble. Either Goran had no heart, or he scientifically fell to avoid a blow.

Whichever it was he had not the pluck to get up again, but lay there glaring at the two.

"I think we had better go," said Jack. "With your permission we will escort you to the end of the lane, and then you will be safe from further insult."

"You go, Jack," said Cecil, "and I will stay here and see that this cad doesn't follow you."

It required a bit of a wrench for him to make this proposal—but he did it, and, as a bit of boyish self-abnegation, it stood pretty well to the front.

Jack and Miss Whymper walked a little way down the field, and went out of it by a gate. Cecil coolly stood over Ned Goran, who at first made no effort to rise.

"If Mr. Bangwell knew of this," said Cecil, "he would kick you out of the house."

"Let him kick me out," whined Goran; "I don't care.'

"So you say now.

"Are you going to tell him anything about it?"

"I think I ought to do so."

"You know you won't," said Goran, sitting up; "it isn't in your line."

"No, it isn't," replied Cecil; "but if ever you insult that girl again—"

"Oh! pooh!" said Goran, contemptuously. "Who wants to insult her—who cares a straw about her? She is as changeable as the wind. The other day I was everything to her, now I'm nothing."

"Goran, mind what you say," said Cecil, turning pale. "You may have to prove your words."

"And I can prove them," said Goran. "I've got letters from her that would show you what good friends we've been. She ain't worth fighting about, or I would have given Jack Wyburn such a trouncing as he never had in his life. He is welcome to her."

Cecil was too agitated to stop him, and Goran, with his hands in his pockets, sauntered away in the opposite direction taken by Jack and the young lady.

Cecil was more miserable than ever now.

He had, in his thoughts, made something of an idol of the girl with the beautiful hair and eyes, and now a rude hand had cast it down. But the idol was not quite shattered.

"I won't believe him," said Cecil, vehemently. "He is a mean, lying sneak. Write to him—it isn't possible."

He did not go immediately after Jack, but lingered awhile, and when he did follow, Jack was not, as he expected, at the end of the lane.

Glancing down the high road, in the direction of Moatborough, he saw him sauntering along by the side of Miss Whymper.

They were walking very slowly, she with her head hanging a little, and Jack with his face towards her.

"Of course," muttered Cecil, "I might have expected it. Heigho! I shall not wait for him."

Anxious to rid himself of the many disagreeable thoughts that bothered him, he hurried off in the direction of a common known as Brindle Heath.

It was about two miles from Moatborough, and, as he knew, the majority of the boys had gone thither.

Breaking into a sharp run he was soon in the neighbourhood, and at a distance observes a host of boys gathered together.

As he drew nearer he saw that some of them were kneeling on the ground, and the majority of those standing by had sticks in their hands.

"After rats," he thought; "hardly the place for them."

But the game in hand was a more ambitious one.

Bob Rudge and Tom Drake had put their money together, and bought a ferret of a travelling tinker, who assured them that it would, in ten minutes, turn out all the rabbits on the common.

"Jest put that ere little critter into a rabbit hole," he said, "and out will come Mister Whitetail."

These facts were imparted to Cecil as soon as he joined the group, and he was furthermore informed by Bob that the ferret had been duly put into a hole, but neither it nor a rabbit had yet come out.

"How long has it been there?" asked Cecil.

"About half an hour," replied Bob.

"Then you won't see it any more to-day," said Cecil, decisively.

"Why not?"

"It's laid up with a rabbit, and it won't leave the hole while there's an ounce of it left."

"But he can't eat it all," said Bob, aghast.

"He will in time," replied Cecil, who was country bred, and knew all about such things. "The only thing is to dig him out."

"But we haven't got a spade."

"Then here you will have to leave him.'

"There he is!" cried one of the boys, excitedly.

The nose of the ferret appeared at the mouth of a burrow. Bob made a grab at it.

In an instant the little beast had fastened on his finger, fortunately only getting hold of the tip of it.

"Oh!" roared Bob.

He jerked back his hand, breaking the skin of his finger, and the ferret disappeared.

"Just your luck, Bob," said Harry Farnborough. "Why didn't you keep hold of him?"

"Oh! you're an idiot," said Bob, actively engaged in sucking his wounded finger.

"It's all right," said Cecil; "the little beggar

hasn't laid up. He's hunting about, that's all. Don't all stand here, but keep your eyes on the burrows around. We may see a rabbit pop out any moment."

The boys immediately spread themselves about, and at least one was posted at every hole in the immediate vicinity.

Bob remained where he was, and having bound his handkerchief about the wound, got ready for active operations.

Cecil took on himself the task of general instructor.

"All keep quiet," he said, "and the moment you see a rabbit strike. Hit forward, about a foot in front of him, and then you may give him one."

It was a time of intense excitement.

The instinct of what is called sport, otherwise the desire to kill, is in us all, more or less, and every boy there was burning to knock a rabbit on the head. None burned so much as Bob.

He felt that he owed the rabbits a grudge for his bitten finger. If they had not kept out of the way he would not have been bitten by the ferret, for the little beast would then have had something else to do.

Bob kept his eagle eyes on the hole, holding the stick at a nice elevation, ready to strike.

Cecil laid down behind him, with his ear to the ground.

"Look out," he whispered, "there's scuffling in the burrow. Be ready."

Out came a head, and Bob brought down the stick with a whack, that stopped the further progress of the creature.

"I've got him," cried Bob.

"Yes, you have," said Cecil, disgusted ; "it's the ferret, and you've killed it."

He dragged out the victim of Bob's prowess, showing that it was indeed the ferret. Bob could have wept

"What beastly luck !" he said, with a moan.

The boys came up laughing, they could not help it, and gathered round Cecil, who was closely examining the dead ferret.

"Don't cry over it, Bob," he said. "You haven't lost much. It was a very old ferret, lame on its fore legs, and as blind as a bat."

CHAPTER XXV.

JACK MAKES A PAINFUL DISCOVERY—A FRUIT-
LESS APPEAL—NOT WANTED.

UR readers will, perhaps, wonder at Jack Wyburn deserting his friend, but few in his place would not have done the same. He found in Miss Whymper a charming companion, and that is all we need say about it.

Having got to the end of the lane, he suggested they should go on together for a little, "just to see her safe out of Goran's reach," and the little became a long way, until Moatborough was in sight.

"We must part now," said Miss Whymper.

She raised her eyes to his in a shy, pretty way, that did more mischief than a bold look would have done.

"Must we ?" asked Jack, softly.

"Yes."

"But we have not finished our conversation."

"What have we been talking about ?"

Jack could not clearly say.

They had been talking about something, and that was all they knew.

The situation was rather ridiculous, and they both laughed.

"Of course we must part," said the young lady, "for it would not do for us to be seen together."

"But I shall see you again, I hope," pleaded Jack.

"I don't know," said Miss Whymper. "Good-bye !"

She gave him her hand—he took it, and then in a moment she was hurrying away, as if eager to get as far as possible from him.

"A pretty girl," said Jack, "but a strange one. She seems offended, and yet I don't know what I've done to wound her susceptibilities."

Ah ! Jack, my boy, the ways of women, which are the same as the ways of girls, are puzzling to us all. The gentle sex are so many walking conundrums, which are never found out.

He turned back, and, remembering where he had left Cecil, hastened to the lane.

Not finding his friend, he went on up its narrow way.

Cecil, as we know, had gone in another direction, and, of course, Jack saw nothing of him. Wandering on he presently came to a bye-road, where there was an inn.

By its outside appearance an expert in such things would have judged it to be the haunt of the idling labourer and the poacher.

On a bench outside sat two persons drinking together. One was of the Gruesum type—he might have been his brother. The other was a respectably clad youth, about Jack's own age, or a little older.

The moment he glanced at the face a cry burst from Jack's lips.

How could he mistake those features.

"Harold Gillispie !" he cried.

The youth looked up, then sprang to his feet and endeavoured to run away.

But he ran as one with fettered limbs, and Jack speedily overtook him.

The boy sank upon his knees, covering his face with his hands.

"I am sorry to find you here," said Jack.

No answer.

The burly ruffian the boy had been drinking with came sauntering up and spoke roughly.

"You let him alone," he said ; "you ain't his master."

"No," replied Jack, sadly, "but I should like to be his friend. Come, Gillispie," he added, addressing the boy, "come away with me. I promise you I won't say a word about it."

The boy bent his head lower, and his body quivered with emotion, but he made no reply.

"If you won't come I can't force you," said Jack, "but do listen to me."

"Can't a young gent have a drop o' liquor without every fool interfering with him?" asked the ruffian. "I call it cheek on your part to worry him."

"My good fellow, I have nothing to say to you," replied Jack, coldly. "For the last time, Gillispie, will you come with me?"

"No," replied the boy, in a low tone.

"Very well," said Jack, sadly, "then I must leave you. One thing you may rely upon. I shall never speak to a soul about what I have seen to-day. Oh! do let me be a friend to you?"

"No—no, go away," was the answer.

Jack still lingered, but the other finally settled the question by suddenly leaping to his feet, casting a hurried glance at him, and rushing into the inn.

"You see," said the loafing ruffian, "he don't want any of your parsoning. You let him alone. Me and him are uncommon good friends."

"I would almost sooner have seen him *dead*," said Jack, passionately. "What is he thinking of —dreaming of—to associate with you?"

"All right, my young cockolorum," said the ruffian, with a grin. "I can 'scuse a bit of tongue from you. Your game is to sponge on him, and you're disappointed."

Jack turned from the brute, and strode quickly away.

Jack was not a milksop, but he despised low company—that is, the company of the depraved. The discovery he had made inexpressibly pained him.

"I see it all now," he muttered. "He is some big swell who has gone wrong, and has been sent to us because his own set won't have anything to do with him. I can't understand him, but in my heart I like the fellow."

Jack went for a long walk across country, and measured the distance so as to be home just before the appointed hour.

Somewhat fatigued, he was glad to get back, and not seeing anyone as he approached the playground he believed he was first back.

But it was not so, for Harold Gillispie was sauntering about the grounds reading a book.

His face was dreadfully pale, and he was undoubtedly troubled.

As Jack entered the playground Harold looked up, recognised him, and walked away.

"Don't go," cried Jack. "Never mind what has happened this afternoon."

"What has happened," demanded Gillispie, adding a moment afterwards, "that concerns you?"

"It is not my affair, of course," said Jack, biting his lip. "I will let it slide."

Jack was deeply hurt, and he was just as angry with himself as he was with Gillispie.

He saw it was no use trying to thrust his friendship on the newcomer, and resolved in future to leave him to himself.

———

CHAPTER XXVI.

BIFFINS AND HIS BELL—A QUARREL AT THE TEA-TABLE—JACK IN THE WRONG FOR ONCE.

EALLY, Ben, I shall never be satisfied until I see him humiliated and kicked out of the school."

It was Ned Goran who spoke thus. He and Ben Chicks were in secret consultation in the playground.

Every moment the bell summoning the boys inside was expected to ring out. No games were going on, for the half-holiday had been a tiring one, and the youngsters stood about in groups talking of the doings of the afternoon.

"It's all very well to talk," replied Ben; "but how are you going to humiliate him?"

"Somehow," replied Goran, darkly. "Of course, you will assist me?"

"Well, that depends upon circumstances," observed Chicks.

"You said you would stand by me through all."

"Yes," returned Chicks; "but I didn't say I would fall with you."

"Not if you can help it," said Goran, bitterly. "You are a good hand at shuffling."

"Mind what you say," returned Chicks, with a snarl.

"Well," said Goran, "I suppose it will not do to quarrel. It would only be playing into the hands of those we hate. You can help me now."

"How?"

"By giving me an idea. You are a good hand at working up mischief."

"I'll think it over," said Chicks. "Perhaps I shall be able to suggest something."

The bell now interrupted them with its melodious clang, and they went into the house with a stream of boys, all ready for their usual late tea-supper of the half-holiday.

On their way to the dining-room they had to pass the bell cupboard.

The door was still open, and Biffins had just left off ringing.

His face was in a profuse state of perspiration, and his breath came hard and short.

"You make a stiff job of that ringing, Biffins," said Chicks.

"I don't mean to have no more complaints about it," replied Biffins. "Mr. Bangwell likes to hear the most made of it."

On entering the room the pair of conspirators, as we may reasonably call them, dropped into seats opposite Jack and Harry Farnborough.

On the evening of half-holidays the fixed routine in the dining-room was abandoned.

The tutors were not always there, and on this occasion they were absent.

The boys had the room to themselves, and were waited on by Biffins and Cobb.

"Now, Shanks," cried Chicks to Biffins, "let us have some tea—smart."

"You come and get it yourself," replied Biffins

• if people call me names I ain't a-going to wait on 'em."

"Hear—hear !" said Cobb.

" *You* keep quiet," said Biffins ; "boys of your age oughtn't to cut in with ' hear—hears,' like a—a member of Parliament."

"Enough," said Cobb, in sepulchral tones ; " I'm done. Tackle the hurn and run out the tea."

The clattering of cups and plates followed. With a good appetite even weak tea and thick bread-and-butter are things not to be despised, especially when accompanied by a few delicacies.

"Goran," suddenly said Chicks, "where have you been to-day ?"

Goran had not confided the story of his humiliation to his friend, and, turning pale, he hesitated before replying.

"Oh ! I strolled about," he said.

"I reckoned you'd gone after—you know who," said Chicks. "I saw her go out."

Goran cast a quick glance at Jack, who was losing colour.

He did not reply.

"You know who I mean—Fanny Maud Whymper," said Chicks.

"Excuse me," interrupted Jack, "but I don't think it right to make that young lady's name a subject for idle chatter."

"Goodness ! What have you to do with it ?" asked Chicks.

"Ask Goran," replied Jack, curtly.

Chicks looked from one to the other with a puzzled face, then suddenly burst out laughing.

"Both gone there," he said. "Ha—ha !"

"Be quiet, will you," said Jack.

"What for ?" asked Chicks. "Look here. She's a pal o' mine, too."

"You lie !" said Jack, rising in his seat. "Be silent or I will make you."

"What is there to be silent about ?" demanded Chicks. "Here's a girl—"

But he got no further.

Jack jumped upon his seat, leant across the table, and gave Chicks an open-handed smack on the face.

"Now will you be quiet ?" he said.

The blow, although it was open-handed, was rather a heavy one, and as it fell upon Chicks' nose the stream of life at once began to flow.

He got up in a hurry, clapped his handkerchief to his face, and hurried from the room.

A perfect uproar ensued.

Angry hisses were heard up and down the table, some taking Jack's part, the others supporting Chicks.

"He hadn't any right to hit him sitting," cried Goran ; " it was mean and cowardly."

"What ! must you say something ?" demanded Jack, fiercely. "Be quiet or I will serve you again as I did this afternoon."

"You struck me *then* when I wasn't looking," yelled Goran.

"Liar !"

"Fool !"

Jack sprang out of his seat, and ran round the table ; some of his friends tried to restrain him, but he tossed them aside as if they had been little children.

Goran also got out of his seat, but not to fight. His intention was to clear out.

"Stop it !"

"Don't let 'em fight !"

"There'll be an awful row over this !" cried the boys, though they did very little else but yell.

Goran made for the door, and Jack ran after him, upsetting Cobb with two cups of tea, thereby endangering the personal safety of that romantic youth.

Luckily the hot tea was thrown on the floor, and nobody was scalded.

Jack sprang at Goran, and had just collared him, when the door opened and Mr. Bangwell came in.

Close behind him was Chicks, still with his handkerchief up to his nose.

"Silence," said the schoolmaster.

He had no need to cry out, for all were quiet enough, and Jack had let go of Ned Goran.

Not a little ashamed now of the heat he had exhibited, he drew back and awaited the reproaches he was sure would be heaped upon him.

"Wyburn," said Mr. Bangwell, "your conduct is disgraceful !"

"I am afraid I forgot myself, sir," replied Jack.

"But what is it all about ?" asked Mr. Bangwell. "You don't quarrel and fight like this for a pastime ?"

"I would rather not tell you what it was about, sir," said Jack.

"It was about nothing," said Chicks. "Goran was talking to me when Wyburn told us to hold our tongues, and because we would not obey him he jumped up and hit me across the table."

"Wyburn," said Mr. Bangwell, "is this the truth ?"

"Let it pass as being true, sir," said Jack. "I have nothing more to say about it."

"Finish your tea," said Mr. Bangwell, abruptly. " I will inflict some punishment upon you to-morrow. Quiet there !"

He took a seat at the head of the table, and remained there until the meal was finished.

The latter end of it was uncommonly quiet. Even whispering was not indulged in.

After tea a short time was sleepily devoted to study, and then they went to bed.

Jack was in a silent frame of mind. He felt very unhappy, for he knew that he had acted harshly, and so played into the hands of his enemies.

Cecil Mead came over and sat down on the side of his bed.

"Jack," he said, "you made an awful mistake to-night."

"I know it," replied Jack, gloomily. "I ought to have waited until we met outside."

"You should not have struck Chicks at all."

"What ! When he was talking in an insulting way about her ?"

"Jack," said Cecil, earnestly, "you know I would not say anything I did not believe to be true."

"I am sure you would not," replied Jack.

"Then you may take this from me as a fact," said Cecil. "Miss Whymper is a regular flirt, and not worth fighting about."

"How do you know ?" asked Jack.

"In many ways," said Cecil, "but I would rather not go into the matter. If you don't believe me go on fighting about her. When she hears of it she will think it great fun."

Jack made no answer, and Cecil, after casting a

wistful look at him, gloomily crossed over to his own couch and prepared for rest.

It was not a night for fun or even talking.

All were tired out, and speedily asleep—save one.

Jack, with open eyes, lay still, thinking over the events of the day, and failing to draw one atom of joy or consolation from anything that had transpired.

Not worth fighting about?

Well! she was very pretty, anyway; and then there was that strange business of Harold Gillispie's.

It was sad, puzzling, vexing, and midnight had passed when Jack found rest from his thoughts in oblivion.

CHAPTER XXVII.
SOME PECULIAR LETTERS.

SAYS the sage: "Time flies; nothing stops or checks it." Man has become so awfully clever that he can do anything almost but stand still, although a fortnight passed away at the school with very little incident to record. Among the minor events we may mention that the mysterious ringer of the bell alarmed and aggravated the house once more, and, as before, remained undiscovered, while Jack had had a brief stolen interview with Miss Fanny Whymper over the wooden fence.

Cobb fell downstairs with Mrs. Bangwell's pet china tea-things, and Bob Rudge, while showing the boys how to box, tripped backwards through the schoolroom window, and the cost of the same was put down to his name.

Ned Goran and Ben Chicks were closer friends than ever, spending much time in talking privately to each other, and between Jack and Cecil there was a slight estrangement.

These are the only matters worth mentioning, and with regard to the latter, it arose through Cecil again warning Jack not to have anything to do with Miss Fanny Whymper.

"Very good advice," said Jack, coolly; "but are you sure it is entirely unselfish? I fancy you do not exactly dislike her."

This made Cecil angry, the more so because he spoke from inward conviction that the girl was a flirt.

Feeling very sure about it, he resolved to go to Ned Goran, and ask to look at the letters he had spoken of.

He hardly expected to be obliged, and was somewhat astonished by the readiness with which his request was complied with.

"Certainly," said Ned. "I have them in my pocket."

He took them out of an old pocket-book he carried, and handed them to Cecil. They were all very short, and one will suffice as a sample of the rest.

"*My darling Ned,—It was kind of you to send me the sweets. I shall be out to-morrow evening with Eva. Hope to see you,—Your loving* "F. M. W."

Cecil felt more pained than he thought he should have done. He was hurt on his own account, and on Jack's also.

"I won't see him mixed up with such a chit," he muttered.

"May I have these letters for a day or two?" he asked.

CHAPTER XXVIII.
MIKE IN TROUBLE.

IF you promise to return the letters I will lend them to you," said Ned Goran.

"Of course I will."

"Then you may have them."

It was with some feeling of doing rather a mean thing that Cecil went to Jack with these letters and asked him to read them.

Jack looked them over calmly, and handed them back.

"Why do you bring this rubbish to me?" he asked.

"Because I don't like to see you hanging about that girl," earnestly replied Cecil. "Believe me, dear Jack, I am acting as I think for the best."

"No doubt," said Jack, severely. "Goran gave you these letters, of course?"

"I asked him for them."

"Same thing. You go and tell him from me that if he says Miss Whymper wrote these letters he lies."

"It is useless to try and help him," murmured Cecil, as he walked sorrowfully away. "I can't exactly blame him. I daresay I should act as he does."

"I say, Cecil," said Harry Farnborough, coming up behind and smacking him on the back.

"Well, what do you want?" tartly asked Cecil.

"Some of us are going down to the river side. Mike Feeley's got a cottage there. We are going to draw him out—like a badger."

"You had better leave him alone. He is a vicious old brute."

"We are not afraid of him. Will you go?"

"Not to-day."

Harry turned away, and a few minutes later he, Bob Rudge, Tom Drake, and two or three more, were on their way to the river, which lay on the south side of the town.

It was Saturday afternoon, and they had a good two hours to spare for "drawing the badger."

The river was called the Crawler, because it ran so slowly, but its real name was the Arrow, because in one part it ran straight for a mile, and then spread out into a broad channel, so as to somewhat resemble that ancient weapon.

A stone bridge spanned it at the foot of the town, and on the opposite bank, about a third of a mile down, stood an old cottage, sheltered by trees and surrounded by a badly kept garden.

Mike Feeley had recently moved in there, and it was his humour to live alone.

He was rarely seen in the town, or anywhere adjacent.

"We've got to go up quietly," said Bob Rudge, "and as soon as we are near enough we must all start singing—

" ' *Come out of your hole, old Mike,*
Your head we'll put on a pike.'

It will be a sort of song, but I don't know any more of it."

"Who made up what you *do* know?" asked Harry Farnborough.

"I did," replied Bob, swelling with pride.

"Out of your own head?"

"Yes."

"Without anybody to help you?"

"Of course."

"Bob," said Harry, with deep emotion, "Tennyson

The umbrella was raised and then descended like the sword of a crusader.

and that inferior lot can now take a back seat. It's brilliant and beautiful."

"Oh! that's coming it too strong," said Bob, glaring at the grinning faces about him; "but can you do anything like it?"

"I wouldn't if I could," replied Harry; "I should expect six months' hard labour for it, and feel I deserved it."

"I call you a hateful, ass!" said Bob, striding on.

Mike Feeley's cottage stood back about twenty yards from the stream, with some waste ground around the garden, where briars and furze grew in abundance.

Bob was so indignant at being chaffed about his "poetry" that he resolved to sing it all alone, and, breaking into a trot, put thirty yards or so between him and his chums.

The gate of the garden was at the side, and thither went Bob. Leaning over it, he began to chant—

"*Come out of your hole, old Mike,*
Your—"

He got no further, for Mike Feeley came out from behind a group of furze bushes just behind him, and without any preliminary nonsense, struck the singer on the head with his clenched fist.

Poor Bob went down and lay quite still, as if he was dead.

Mike Feeley looked hurriedly around, and, catching sight of the other boys, turned livid.

"If you come near me," he cried, "I'll kill every man Jack of you!"

"Come on," said Harry; "he's not going to do as he likes with Bob."

Whether Mike Feeley was afraid or not, he thought it prudent to retire, and the boys picked up Bob, who, beyond breathing heavily, showed no sign of life.

"Let's carry him to the river and bathe his face," suggested Tom Drake.

"As good a thing as can be done," assented Harry.

As they picked up Bob he gave a convulsive twitch and opened his eyes.

"What are you doing?" he asked. "Come—none of your larks."

"Mike Feeley knocked you down," replied Tom Drake.

"So he did," said Bob. "Let go of me. I'm all right, except a sort of burning in my head. Where is the old beast?"

"Gone indoors."

"Then I'll have him out again."

Bob looked round him for a missile of some sort, and saw an old heavy iron kettle, which had been cast out from the cottage with some other rubbish.

"Just the thing!" he said.

Picking it up, he opened the garden gate, and before the others could fairly grasp his intentions he sent it through the ground-floor window of the cottage.

It was a lead-latticed window, and Bob fairly knocked in one side of it.

It was a perfect piece of destructive work in its way.

The next moment Mike Feeley was outside with a huge club-stick in his hand, and the boys had to run, or without doubt he would have murdered some of them in his mad rage.

As it was he pursued them right into the town, and the inhabitants were edified by the sight of a flying body of boys, pursued by a maddened, vicious old man.

Now it happened that Mr. and Mrs. Bangwell were in the High-street, looking at the shops, and making sundry purchases of fruit and grocery, when Bob Rudge, heading the flying party by consent, turned a corner sharply, and ran full butt against Mr. Bangwell, just as he was receiving a bag of oranges from an obsequious greengrocer.

So violent was the collision that Bob flew back and fell into a sitting position, and Mr. Bangwell, in his alarm, tossed the bag of oranges into the air. His hat also fell off.

Then round came the other boys, narrowly escaping a general pantomimic tumble over the prostrate Bob.

"Boys," cried Mr. Bangwell, "what is the meaning of this unseemly conduct?"

"Oh! it's nothing," said Mrs. Bangwell, sarcastically. "They are only having a bit of fun."

Mr. Bangwell was about to say something more, when Mike Feeley came panting round the corner.

The old man was pretty well blown, and hardly in fighting trim.

"Oh! I see," said Mr. Bangwell. "The boys are flying from this man's violence. Stand back, you old scoundrel!"

"I'll kill 'em all!" gasped Mike—"every one. I'll brain 'em—smash 'em!"

"Stand off, I say," said Mr. Bangwell, putting himself between old Mike and the boys. "Police!"

"Well, let 'em come," said old Mike, suddenly calm, "and I'll give 'em in charge."

"What for?"

"Smashing my windows."

"Is it true what he says?" asked Mr. Bangwell.

"He hit me with his fist first, sir," cried Bob. "Here, on the side of my head."

In proof of it Bob offered for the inspection of the schoolmaster a bump as big as half a hen's egg —quite a little marvel in the way of swellings.

A number of people had now gathered around, and a policeman put in an appearance. He at once went for Mike Feeley.

"What are you doing now?" he asked.

"One of my pupils has been dreadfully assaulted," said Mr. Bangwell. "Rudge, let the officer see that protuberance on your head. It is the work of that violent-tempered old man."

The officer professionally examined Bob's head, and, addressing Mr. Bangwell, said—

"You had better summon him, sir. Most likely he'll be sent to prison."

"Send me to prison!" cried Mike, with eyes that seemed to shoot forth small lightning flashes. "You daren't!"

"Boys," said Mr. Bangwell, with dignity, "go home. Officer, see that they are not molested. I've dropped my hat."

"Is this it?" asked a baker's man, offering the schoolmaster a flattened *chapeau*. "Sorry to say I walked right atop of it."

"You ought to have been more careful," said Mr. Bangwell. "Dear me! I'm afraid it's entirely spoiled."

"Well, walk home without one," whispered Mrs. Bangwell, "and don't stand there for everybody to gape and grin at you!"

"My dear," said Mr. Bangwell, in an undertone, "this is hardly the language for the public ear."

"Oh ! bother," she answered ; "never mind the hat. Put it down as broken windows in the boys' bills. It won't be for the first time !"

The boys had already gone on, and Mr. Bangwell, fearing further revelations from Mrs. Bangwell, who had lost her temper over the affair, hastened in the same direction.

Mike Feeley, regardless of the gaping assembly around him, stood still, watching the retreating schoolmaster with an evil face.

"Send me to prison !" he muttered ; "you had better do it, if you dare. If once I'm sent there I'll go a second time for *something that people will talk about !*"

"Here, get along ! Don't stand there blocking up the path," said the officer, giving him a push.

"Hands off !" hissed Mike.

"Get along with you !"

Another push.

Then the knobbed stick was raised and descended with terrific force on the head of the officer, crushing his helmet in, and making him see as many stars as two eyes were capable of looking at.

The officer was a plucky fellow, and closed with him at once.

A fierce struggle followed ; but Mike's great strength was overcome by science, and, handcuffed, he was led away to prison.

CHAPTER XXIX.

COBB HAS A SUNDAY OUT.

MIKE FEELEY, for his assault on the police, was sentenced to fourteen days' imprisonment, which arranged matters so that he would be liberated about the same time as Buck Gruesum. Moatborough could do very well without them for a time, and it may be said that everybody drew more or less satisfaction from their incarceration.

To Sam Barlow it was a matter of great delight. Between him and them no love was lost.

He almost took a drop of his old enemy in his exultation ; but, happily, did not go so far.

Had he done so, the usual result would have ensued—a fresh breaking out in the wrong direction, for he was one of those men who find it difficult to be moderate in the matter of drinking.

About this time Mr. Bangwell gave Cobb a rise in life—not in wages, but in headgear.

Instead of the cap he had hitherto worn, a tall hat, with gold lace, was provided for him—a fearful and wonderful thing in the way of *chapeaux*.

Cobb had a liking for anything to distinguish him from the common world, and this hat gave him boundless delight.

He managed to convey to 'Melia the tidings of his additional adornment, and hinted that if she could get out next Sunday afternoon he would meet her near the post-office.

"*We will have a walk together,*" he wrote, "*and yule find me got up in a way not to be ashamed on.*"

Now 'Melia seldom got a holiday of any sort ; but recently she had been let loose on Sunday afternoon for the purpose of attending a school attached to a mission-hall.

This gave her an opportunity to see the gallant Cobb ; but to enjoy his alluring society she must play truant from that school.

It was a desperate and daring thing to do ; but as Miss Fillwell was an Episcopalian, she would know very little of what went on at the mission-hall, and, therefore, there was a chance of 'Melia's back-sliding not being discovered.

Sunday afternoon came, and Cobb, in what may be called, "crowning glory," started out.

He felt that it was a great occasion, and the eye of the public would be on him.

And it fell upon him accordingly.

But, strange to say—they laid it to the Bangwell boys—reverence for old institutions was dying out at Moatborough, and Cobb's hat, instead of exciting admiration, brought upon him a fire of criticism from the boys.

"Oh ! my," said one, "ain't he smart. How's the Lady Mayoress ?"

"If I put a hat like that on *my* head," said another, "I should expect to be locked up as a baby frightener."

"He won it at a raffle !" exclaimed a third.

Cobb was a bit taken aback by the feeling he excited ; but his lofty pride came to his aid, and with his head erect and eyes flashing with scorn, he wended his way to the post-office.

'Melia was there before him, and Cobb saluted her by raising his hat with a flourish.

This act of gallantry was recognised by the boys with a derisive cheer.

"A low lot !" said Cobb. "Come on, 'Melia."

He offered her his arm, and off they went.

Common prudence ought to have prompted him to get into the country ; but Cobb was determined that the Moatborough people should see his hat, and strode down the High-street.

The boys followed behind in a state of high glee. It was a treat for them, but a greater joy was to come.

Miss Fillwell was out visiting the poor, and as she was walking up one of the bye-streets she saw Cobb and 'Melia go by.

The sight, for a moment, petrified her.

'Melia was her slave, and Cobb she loathed, not only as the henchman of Mr. Bangwell, but as a boy possessed of qualities which were repulsive to her.

He was impudent and vulgar. He had openly derided her.

Recovering herself, she went upon the trail.

The boys saw her coming, and backed a little so that she could come up immediately behind the tender pair.

She was not going to waste words upon them, but bring about a severence by striking them a blow with her umbrella.

By bringing it down upon their linked arms she could do it.

The umbrella was raised and then descended like the sword of a crusader.

But at the very same instant Cobb bent over to whisper a few encouraging words to 'Melia, and the umbrella, instead of striking their arms, descended upon his hat.

It was a prodigious blow.

Miss Fillwell was thin but she was wiry, and the force she put into the blow fairly settled that hat.

Furthermore, it nearly settled Cobb, and entirely scattered the wits of 'Melia.

They staggered apart, Cobb falling against the wall of an adjoining house, and 'Melia clinging to a lamp-post.

"Go home, you abandoned girl!" said Miss Fillwell, in her most commanding tone. "How dare you walk about with a low boy?"

Poor 'Melia had no answer but her tears to give; but Cobb, having recovered himself a little, showed fight.

"So it's you, is it, Miss Bag-o-bones?" he said. "Where's the perlice? You can't hammer people in this way without being locked up!"

"You little villain!" cried Miss Fillwell. "I'll have you whipped."

"You'll get into trouble about this hat," said Cobb. "Don't you think I'm going to pick up the ruins of it. Master gave one pound ten for it."

Miss Fillwell had taken 'Melia by the arm and was marching her off by this time. Cobb picked up the battered hat and followed.

"I mean to lock yer up," he said, "but, in course, there's no perlice about on Sunday. You're a most wiolent old woman. I pities poor 'Melia, I do."

"Go away, you saucy little ruffian!" said Miss Fillwell.

It was a time of trouble to her, for there was quite a stream of people on their way to St. Peter's Church for afternoon service, and people stared, as well they might, at the strange spectacle of an aged female leading a weeping girl, with a boy carrying a battered hat behind; without speaking of the contingent of the delighted idlers.

"What do you mean by coming up behind and breaking of my hat?" said Cobb, raising his voice. "I never did nothing to you. It looks like drinking."

"WILL you go away?" hissed Miss Fillwell, turning sharply upon him.

"No," answered Cobb. "Not till this hat's paid for. I ought to have locked you up the last time you 'saulted me with a pail of water. You are allus going on like a madwoman. I asks the gineral public to look at this 'ere hat."

The public looked at it, and the public grinned or smiled according to their social positions. Miss Fillwell felt her blood boiling within her.

"If you don't go away," she said, "I'll kill you."

"Do it," said Cobb, defiantly. "Nothin' would please me better than to see you hung. Why—"

But here Cobb was checked by the sight of his master and mistress on their way to church.

They both stared at the wondrous scene, and Cobb began his story. But Mr. Bangwell stopped him.

"Go home, Cobb," he said. "I see you have again been subjected to maltreatment from one who ought to know better. Go home!"

Miss Fillwell had already stalked on, dragging the hapless 'Melia with her. Cobb again went in pursuit.

He did not, however, say anything more until they were nearly home, when he drew up to the side of Miss Fillwell, and said—

"You ain't going to make 'Melia pay for this, I tell you."

Miss Fillwell cast a hasty glance around.

The idlers had all fallen away. Nobody was in sight.

She and Cobb were practically alone, for 'Melia hardly counted.

The vials of her wrath were overflowing, and, swift as an eagle pounces on its prey, she fell upon Cobb.

Let us draw a veil over the scene.

It was a big struggle, for Cobb fought gallantly, but bone and muscle were against him.

Defeat fell to his lot.

Battered about out of shape, he was left sitting in the roadway by Miss Fillwell, who, with her bonnet all awry, and a torn and dishevelled dress, retreated to her abode, satisfied in one respect, but hardly pleased with the afternoon's performance, as a whole.

CHAPTER XXX.

SOMETHING WRONG SOMEWHERE—JACK AND THE STRANGE PUPIL—WHO STOLE THE WATCH?

COBB expected great things would come out of his adventure with Miss Fillwell, but to his great disgust the matter was hushed up.

Perhaps it was as well for both parties that Miss Fillwell thought proper to apologise for her "temporary excitement," and offered to purchase a new hat for Cobb.

Mr. Bangwell had his reasons for accepting the apology and the offer, and so the matter dropped.

When Cobb heard it he said, bitterly—

"Let it be thusly—and she may dream on in fancied se—cu—ri—ty; but the hand of the avenger niver sleeps."

He told his story to the boys, garnished with flowers of rhetoric culled from the garden of romance, and they incited Cobb to be speedy with his vengeance.

This he promised to do, and fell back into his usual life's routine.

A few days later there was a deal of whispering among the boys—a series of confidential communications between chums.

This state of things arose from the discovery that there was a thief in the school.

All sorts of little valuables had disappeared ; but as their intrinsic value was not much nobody cared to make a public complaint.

Ned Goran said he had lost a silver pencil-case, " once the property of his mother," and Ben Chicks whispered of certain " old coins " which had been taken from his box.

Neither the pencil-case nor the coins had ever been seen by the boys, and had the presumed losers stopped there nobody would have thought much about them. But there were other complaints which could not be ignored.

Tom Drake had lost a gold seal from his box, and Harry Farnborough missed two shillings in money. There were about half a score other little losses which could not have been trumped up.

It was not often that a suggestion from Ben Chicks was accepted, but when he advised that the boys should hold a private meeting about it everybody fell in with the idea.

To keep the matter as quiet as possible, it was decided to hold it in the schoolroom in the evening, at an hour when they were usually left to themselves.

Everybody was anxious to get at the bottom of the bad business, and there was nearly a full muster at the time appointed.

The only absentee was Harold Gillispie.

As Ben Chicks had suggested the meeting, he was voted to the chair, and at once entered on the business.

Taking a piece of paper from his pocket, he said—

" I have been round the school quietly to get a list of the things that are missing, and before we do anything else I will read it out to see if it is correct."

We need not give the list here, but it amounted to over a score of articles of varied value which had evidently been stolen. The list was proved to be correct.

" Now comes the question," said Chicks, as he refolded the paper, " who is the thief ?"

A dead silence followed.

The boys looked at each other, but on no face was there the least sign of guilt.

" I would like to suggest," said Ned Goran, " that an open confession might be made, and, on the restoration of the things, nothing more be said about it."

" As if the thief is likely to confess !" exclaimed Jack.

" Why not ?"

" Why not ! Would you, if you were the thief, confess ? Anyway, it would be the fellow's ruin. No, we've got to find out who it is."

" How ?" asked Ben Chicks.

" Ah ! that is more than I can tell you," said Jack.

" By-the-way," said one of the lower-class boys, named Benson, " does anybody know how the new fellow spends his time ? He seems to go out a great deal."

" In other words," said Chicks, " does anybody know anything against him ?"

Nobody knew anything against him but Jack, and he held his tongue. Why he did so, he could not tell, for matters looked rather dark against Gillispie.

" It would never do to judge anyone without absolute proofs," he said.

" That's all right enough," replied Chicks ; " but if I lose anything more I shall go to Bangwell."

" So shall I," responded Ned Goran.

" Why not go now ?" suggested Jack. " I see no reason why we should not. It is a matter that ought to be fathomed and settled."

It was generally agreed that if any more robberies took place, Mr. Bangwell should be consulted in the matter ; and the meeting broke up with a sense of general depression.

The next morning, when the boys were at breakfast, they received a message that they were to go to the class-room immediately after the meal.

As this meant a curtailment of the usual half-hour's play, and none of them remembering its having been cut off before, the boys saw that something very unusual was pending.

After breakfast, they walked quietly to the place appointed, and found Mr. Bangwell—with a very grave face—awaiting them.

" You need not take your usual seats, boys," he said, " but just fall in around me."

They did so in a rough semi-circle, and, the two ushers having arrived, the door was closed.

" Boys," said Mr. Bangwell, " I have a very serious matter to talk about. A robbery has been committed in this house. It appears to me that somebody within the house is the thief."

" Mrs. Bangwell's watch," he went on, after a short pause, " has been stolen. By a mistake she left it last night on the sitting-room table, and this morning it was gone."

This was indeed serious, and many a young cheek grew pale. But there was not a sign of guilt in any face.

Mr. Bangwell was compelled to admit that, as he glanced from one to the other.

" I have already questioned the servants," he said, " and I have no reason to suspect any one of them. Boys, if the thief is among you, I implore him to confess. For the sake of his fellows let this matter be cleared up."

Nobody stirred.

" If not here, then," said Mr. Bangwell, " perhaps he will do so privately. I shall be in my study for the next twenty minutes. You are at liberty to go out-doors for a short time."

He descended from his desk, from which point of vantage he had addressed them, and walked abruptly from the room.

On his way out he motioned to the two ushers to follow him.

There was a tumult of voices as the boys trooped into the playground.

All sorts of suggestions were made and theories advanced about the way to catch the thief.

But who was the thief ?

" I noticed that Harold Gillispie wasn't there," said Harry Farnborough ; " of course, he is excepted from suspicion."

" I don't see why he should be," said Bob Rudge. " It is those quiet fellows who generally do such things."

" Indeed !" said somebody behind him.

Bob turned round, and there was Gillispie, with his hands in his pockets, looking calmly about him.

But he did not look at Jack.

" I have heard of the robbery," he said, " a d have

given Bangwell my word that I know nothing whatever about it. He is satisfied, and I hope you are."

There was, at least, a dozen boys gathered around him, but not one for the moment answered.

"I think we ought to take your word," said Jack, hesitatingly.

"Oh! of course," said several boys, loudly.

Gillispie looked quietly about him, and a faint smile wreathed itself about his lips.

"I see how it is," he said. "You suspect *me*. Well! do as you please, but I am *not* the thief."

With the utmost composure he turned aside, and, with his hands in his pockets, sauntered off to the gate.

"Cool," said Harry Farnborough.

"Oh! he's got the cheek of—of—anyone," said Bob.

"I wish I had taken his word more emphatically," said Jack. "I do not think he is the thief."

"You are right," said Ned Goran, joining the group, "he is not the thief. The things are found, and Mr. Bangwell would like to see you at once, please."

———

CHAPTER XXXI.

A PAINFUL INTERVIEW—UNDER A CLOUD.

ACK noticed there was a ring of triumph in Ned Goran's voice, but apparently paid no heed to it.

With a quiet air he walked into the house, without so much as looking at one of his chums.

He had done nothing wrong, and yet he feared some great evil was impending.

Somehow he was to be associated with the things that had been stolen. Matters were worse, far worse, than he expected.

On entering the study he found Mr. Bangwell grave unto sternness, and Mrs. Bangwell standing behind his chair with unmistakable signs of being deeply troubled.

"Wyburn," said Mr. Bangwell, "a very serious discovery has been made. Did you leave your box in your bedroom unlocked this morning?"

"I left it open," replied Jack, after a moment's consideration. "I was in a great hurry."

"That is how I found it," said Mrs. Bangwell.

"To come to the point," continued Mr. Bangwell, "acting upon the suggestion of—of one of the establishment, Mrs. Bangwell decided to examine some of the boxes and trunks belonging to the boys—"

"May I ask who suggested it?" interposed Jack.

"I have promised not to tell you," said Mr. Bangwell. "Acting on this suggestion, the examination was made—with the result that a parcel was found in your box."

"Indeed, sir!" said Jack, with compressed lips.

"Here it is," continued the schoolmaster, producing a small brown-paper parcel.

Unfolding it, he disclosed a variety of articles—pencil-cases, penknives, small pieces of jewellery, and a watch.

"Now, can you explain how these things came into your box?" asked Mr. Bangwell.

"No, indeed, sir," replied Jack, very white and quiet.

"Or offer any suggestion?"

"I can do that, sir. Somebody—the real thief—has put them there."

"Wyburn," said Mr. Bangwell, "I beseech you not to take refuge in a false accusation, even against somebody unknown."

"I must do so," said Jack, "because I am not a thief, and I did not put the things into my box."

"Well, if you do not confess," returned Mr. Bangwell, "I must deal very sternly with you. You will remain here until after morning studies, and then I will let you know my decision."

"Very well, sir," said Jack, drearily.

He was engaged in turning over the things in a slow, mechanical way, as if he hardly knew what he was doing. Suddenly his eye lighted up.

"All the things said to be lost are not here," he said.

"What of that?" asked Mr. Bangwell.

"Oh! I don't know that it matters," said Jack, very quiet again.

"But you must have had some object in making that remark."

"I thought of something, sir; but it doesn't matter."

"Do you suggest that somebody has been robbing *you?*"

"No, sir; I would rather not say anything more about it at present."

The school-bell at that moment began to ring, and Mr. Bangwell rose from his seat.

"You will not attempt to mix with the other boys, I hope," he said; "at least, not until I tell you?"

"No," answered Jack, "of course not. How could I, with such a stigma forced upon me?"

"Perhaps two or three hours' reflection will assist you in deciding what to do," said Mr. Bangwell; "the more open one is to admit your guilt."

"It is not open to me," replied Jack, with sudden pride, "for I am not guilty."

Mr. Bangwell left the room, but Mrs. Bangwell lingered.

"You have a mother, Wyburn," she said; "for her sake do something so that this dreadful thing may be kept from her."

"What am I to do?"

"Confess."

"That would be lying."

"Now, Wyburn," said Mrs. Bangwell, shaking her head, "do you think it likely that anyone would place things in your box so as to fasten a false suspicion upon you?"

"It is not only likely," replied Jack, "but it has been done."

Mrs. Bangwell sighed as she walked slowly to the door.

"Things are worse than I thought," she said. "You are very young to be so hardened."

Jack made no rejoinder, and, shaking her head again, she left him.

Jack was as one half-stunned.

In a dumb way he knew he had been hit hard, and by-and-bye would feel it worse, and the knowledge of the blow would not be kept from his friends,

"What will mother think?" he murmured. "She who has suffered so, and done so much for me. But she won't—she can't believe me to be *guilty*."

Mere words did not help him.

He felt that the evidence was against him and the difficulty *not* to believe would be very great.

And yet he felt sure about the real culprits.

"This is the work of Ned Goran and Ben Chicks," he muttered, as he paced to and fro. "The things they say they lost *are not here*. They never had them. It was all part of the trickery that has brought me to this.

"But I can't prove it," he went on, as he began playing nervously on the window-pane with his fingers, "and it would be useless to suggest it. I should only make matters worse.

He had nothing to do, and would have been thankful even if he had his usual studies to attend to.

Very likely Mr. Bangwell left him idle so that he might have time to reflect.

There were no books in the study, except a few valuable ones in a case under lock and key, and Jack was finding the position almost insupportable when Cobb came into the room.

He came in with a flourish and humming a tune. Seeing Jack he stopped short.

"Beg parding," he observed, "I didn't know as you was here."

"I am taking a rest, Cobb," said Jack.

"Yes, I know. Rest and wait till master comes along with the cane," said Cobb, mysteriously. "Private whackings is allus the worst, because there's no evidence to prove how thick it's laid on. What yer been doing?"

"Nothing," replied Jack. "I am suffering under a false accusation."

"Ah! I see," said Cobb. "A conspiracy to ruin a noble knight. But never mind, Master Wyburn. True innerence never suffered yet."

"I don't know about that," returned Jack.

"Give me the pertiklers," said Cobb, "and let me fathom the mystery."

"No, I won't trouble you," answered Jack, laughing; "it's kind of you, all the same."

"By the way, Mister Wyburn," said Cobb, "I've got a bit o' news for you. It's of interest to me, if nobody else."

"Well! what is it, Cobb?" asked Jack, expecting to hear he had got a rise in wages, or something akin to it.

"Melia's run away," answered Cobb, in a whisper. "Left Miss Bag-o-bones this morning—hearly. Supposed to hav' been helped by somebody, and *she was*. Ha—ha! I'll trust thee 'll not betray the secret."

"You may, Cobb," said Jack. "Where's she gone to?"

"That I've sworn not to tell," replied Cobb, in deep, tragic tones; "but the maiden is well cared for—well cared for, once again. Ha—ha!"

"But what about, Miss Fillwell," said Jack. "*She will* find out where she is?"

"Let her," returned Cobb, scornfully; "she daren't do anything. She'd a been feeding that poor gal on what wouldn't keep a mouse. If she don't mind I'll put the Society for the Prevention of Cruelty to Ani— I mean for the Abolition of— No, you know what I mean?"

"Oh! it's all right," observed Jack.

"Mum's the word, you know," said Cobb, mysteriously. "Breathe not a syllabub that one so humble as I am in the mysterious affair."

CHAPTER XXXII.

JACK HAS A LAST CHANCE GIVEN HIM—DOWN BY THE RIVER—VERY STRANGE CONDUCT.

JACK nodded, and Cobb, after another signal expressive of the need of secresy, left the room. Somehow this interview, ridiculous as it was in some respects, raised Jack's spirits.

More than half of the gloom he felt before was dispelled, and he even went so far as to walk up and down the room with a smile upon his face.

What, indeed, could Cobb have to do with Jack's affairs, and why should he have anything to do with raising his spirits? More, perhaps, than Jack thought for, as we shall presently see.

Later on, when pressed by Mr. Bangwell to confess, Jack Wyburn replied—

"I have nothing to confess."

That was all he had to say in response to Mr. Bangwell.

The schoolmaster was much distressed by this answer, in a measure, it must be admitted, on his own account.

It was clear now that Jack must be dismissed from the school, and the story, if it got about, would be very damaging to the place.

He was also sorry for Jack.

During an interview with the boy at noon—the final interview," as he called it—he pointed out what a distressing thing it would be for Mrs. Wyburn.

"You know, my dear boy," said Mr. Bangwell, "that your home is darkened by a man who is dissolute. I do not wish to say too much about him, because he is your father; but you are aware that such is the case."

"Indeed, I am!" said Jack, with a sigh.

"From the darkness of a home, made unutterably miserable by your misguided father," said Mr. Bangwell, "your mother looks in one direction for light and comfort. Towards whom does she turn her eyes?"

"To me," said Jack.

"Yes," said Mr. Bangwell, "to you. You are her hope. In you she looks for compensation. In you she hopes to find the qualities that shall atone for your father's misconduct. What will she say when she learns why you have been sent away from here?"

"Must she know?" asked Jack, quickly.

"She must. How is it to be kept from her?"

"It will kill her, Mr. Bangwell."

"Confess, and you shall be forgiven."

"I have nothing to confess," said Jack. "I am incapable of theft."

"But the things were found in your box," urged the schoolmaster.

"Somebody placed them there," said Jack, "and I could easily guess who did it."

"If you can bring evidence against anyone do

so," said the schoolmaster, "but I will not listen to insinuations."

"I name no one," returned Jack. "I simply say I am not guilty."

"One last chance I give you," said Mr. Bangwell. "Take the afternoon to consider your position. Go out for a stroll, and in some quiet place meditate upon your case. On your return write me a line, saying what you will do. If you adhere to your present resolution, pack your box, and I will arrange for you to go home by the evening train."

"Very well, sir," said Jack.

He was weary of the whole thing.

His position appeared so hopeless that he felt like a man condemned to die without any hope of reprieve.

He could only face his lot and make the best of it. Some dinner was sent to him in the solitude of the study, but he scarcely tasted it. He had not the appetite of the hardened criminal, and could not partake of food immediately before his execution. Practically he was shortly to be executed.

He was about to be cast off from his little world and its many joys.

The place and the friends he had there would know him no more.

If they thought of him or talked of him at all, it would be as one *dead!*

Then he thought of somebody with the bright eyes and beautiful hair.

What would she think of it all?

Perhaps she would believe he was innocent; but for all that they would be parted, and might never meet again.

He would have no opportunity of giving her an assurance of his innocence, nor could he do so to the boys.

The morning had been dull, and now it was raining, so that his school-chums could not, as usual, go out to play.

Jack stood by the window, looking at the empty ground, and the spectacle was only another source of misery.

A little later on the rain ceased, but it was too near school-time for the boys to take advantage of the returning sunshine. He could hear them wending their way to the schoolroom.

It struck him that they were quieter than usual. There was less talking, and no sounds of subdued horseplay, as there generally had been.

It seemed as if the shadow of the theft lay upon all.

Or perhaps they were thinking of him, and were sorry?

Well, some would be, of course, but others would rejoice.

No man or boy is entirely popular—the best of us have enemies in our little circle.

Jack waited until the boys were all in, and then, sauntering into the hall, he put on his cap and left the house.

He had to go for a quiet walk and think. The best place for thinking was down by the river.

So thither he went, avoiding the broader thoroughfares of the town, for he felt as if everyone by this time knew that he was accused of theft.

Conscious innocence did not help him as it is supposed to do. It seldom does. The chains of false accusation are very galling to the victim.

The day was fine again, and the country beyond the river looked very fresh and beautiful after the rain.

He thought it was charming—more charming than it had ever been before.

The feeling arose, in fact, from the knowledge that he was about to leave it—for ever, as he believed.

Sad enough, and yet, strange to say, not so miserable as he had been, he sauntered along the river bank on the far side from the town.

No boats were about—there seldom were until the evening, and then only in the summer-time—and for a considerable distance he had the path to himself.

From a perfect well of deep thought he was aroused by a cry for help from the distance.

It was a boy's voice, he thought, as he stopped to listen, not being fully assured of the direction from whence it came.

A repetition of it soon reached his ears. It came from the river's-bank higher up, and just beyond a clump of alder trees.

It was a wild, despairing cry of one in great pain or mortal terror.

Jack ran on in the direction of it, only stopping to drag a hedge-stake from the fence of the foot-path, thinking he might need it.

Passing the alder trees he came in view of the cause of the outcry.

A burly ruffian-looking fellow was kneeling by the river's brink ducking a boy under the water.

He was dragging him to and fro, and pushed his head below the stream in a jerky fashion, just in the way some women treat linen when washing it.

In this fellow Jack recognised the ruffian he had seen drinking at the inn with Harold Gillispie.

Was it Harold whom he was now maltreating?

He bore down upon the pair, and as he drew near he heard the ruffian crying—

"I'll teach 'ee to try your scurvy tricks on me—a-borrowing money on a watch as wasn't silver. Why, durn 'ee! I'll drown 'ee."

Jack was perceived by the fellow before he was fairly upon him, and, dragging the boy out of the river, he cast him down upon the towing-path.

The boy was not dead, or nearly so, for he immediately got upon his feet and turned his face towards Jack.

"Harold!" cried Jack. "Tell me, for mercy's sake, what does this mean?"

But the boy did not answer him.

Having shaken his fist at the ruffian, he darted away, leaving Jack in a state of utter amazement.

"Oh! he be a nice 'un," growled the ruffian; "a-palling up with a cove, and talking about his being rich, and then doing a swindle on him."

"What did he do?" asked Jack.

"He's been wi' me on the drink a bit," said the man, "and stood shot for shot right enough at first. Then he run short, and asks me to lend him ten bob on his watch. I got it for him, and it's a *tin* one, as I am a sinner!"

"For all that," said Jack, "you had no right to attempt to drown him."

"I warn't a-drowning of him," growled the fellow. "I was a simply *washing the rogue out of him.* Look here, I'm a poacher, but I ain't a thief. I'm rough, but I stands to a pal, and when I find one as isn't, I'm down on him."

THE
BANGWELL BOYS

BEING THE SEQUEL TO

Hardiboy James; or, Chums and Chappies.

"Help! push here!" cried Harry.

Jack walked on. He could not interfere any further.

"Harold is in the wrong," he said, to himself. "He should act fairly by his companions, even if he does pick low company."

Nothing more of any moment occurred during his stroll.

He remained by the river till half-past four, and then went back to the school-house.

Nothing helpful had come out of his meditations.

All he had to do was to write a few words to Mr. Bangwell, telling him he had nothing more to say, then pack his trunk, and get ready to leave.

He was back before school was over, with five minutes to spare, but he met one of the pupils in the hall.

It was Harold Gillispie, who had just come down-stairs in dry clothes, cool and unconcerned.

His face brightened a little when he saw Jack, and, taking one of his hands out of his pocket, he laid it on Jack's shoulder, saying—

"*I* don't believe you are a thief."

"Thank you," said Jack. "I shall consider you have squared matters now."

"What matters?" asked Gillispie.

"Oh! I don't want to speak about it, but surely you've not forgotten this afternoon?"

"I don't know what you mean," coolly replied Gillispie.

And with a nod he walked away, softly whistling.

"What a strange fellow!" thought Jack; "but he is right. I ought not to have mentioned it. Now to my packing."

Before doing that he slipped into the study, and wrote on a piece of paper—

"*I have nothing more to say, sir.*'

Having placed it in an envelope, and directed it, he hurried upstairs to put his box in order for leaving.

CHAPTER XXXIII.

COBB IS PROFOUNDLY AGITATED—HE COMES TO THE FRONT AS A WITNESS—NED GORAN IN A FIX.

ERE, what's this?" said Cobb. "Master Wyburn going away?"

Cobb had been aroused from the perusal of a fine old romance, "The Mud-larks of Messbury; or, the Gory Gang of the River," by a remark made by Biffins.

"I was talking to cook," answered the serving man.

"You said Master Wyburn's going," insisted Cobb.

"So I did—what then?"

"What's he going for?"

"Because he's been a stealing."

"Doing *what?*" cried Cobb.

"Stealing watches and trinkets," said Biffins. "They were all found in a brown paper parcel in his box this morning."

"A brown paper parcel?" cried Cobb, pricking up his ears.

"Yes, by missus, at breakfast time. It's a clear case. He's got to go."

"Has he?" said Cobb, hurriedly folding up the journal he was reading. "We'll see about that."

"What can you do in it?" asked Biffins, scornfully.

"What can I do?" cried Cobb, striking a defiant attitude; "why avenge the innocent, and bring the murderer to justice!"

"There's no murderer in it," said Biffins.

"He's as bad," cried Cobb.

"Who's he?"

"Wait and see, Biffins old man. I don't want you to cut in and rob me of the glory of this triumphant hour."

"Books have driven you silly," said the cook.

"Have they?" replied Cobb. "Wait a bit. I'll return anon. Ha—ha! villain! I have thee on the hip."

With striking dramatic action Cobb strode across the kitchen, waved his hand patronisingly to Biffins and the cook, and disappeared.

"He's gone clean daft," said Biffins.

But Cobb was sane enough. It was only his way of putting things.

Straight up to the sitting-room he went, and knocked at the door.

"Come in!" cried Mrs. Bangwell.

Cobb entered the room and found himself in the presence of his master and mistress, who gazed enquiringly at him.

"Ladies and gentlemen," he said, "I beg parding—sir and missus. I've got something to say about Mister Wyburn being accused of stealing. I know all about—"

"Now, Cobb," said Mr. Bangwell, warningly. "be careful what you say."

"I mean to be, sir," replied Cobb. "Perhaps you'd like to swear me. I'm ready to kiss the book."

"Never mind that," said Mrs. Bangwell; "let us hear what you have to say."

"I've only just now heerd that Mister Wyburn's going," said Cobb; "also—what for—and likewise it's through a brown paper parcel found in his box."

"Yes—yes," said Mrs. Bangwell, impatiently.

"Missus," said Cobb, "I saw that parcel placed there."

Cobb put as much dramatic force as he could into these few words, and the result was satisfactory to him. Both Mr. and Mrs. Bangwell jumped from their chairs.

"Go on, Cobb," said the schoolmaster; "tell us all about it."

"This morning," said Cobb, "just before break-fast, I runs up to my room, and—not to deceive you, sir—I admit it was to put some of my books away, the housemaid having a habit of collaring—I mean-taking—'em to light the fires with. Well, ladies and gentlemen—sir and mum—I goes up very quietly, and I comes down very quietly, through it not being regular for me to go up there at that hour, and just as I comes to the bottom of the stairs I sees a form stealing towards the dormitory occupied by Master Wyburn and others of that ilk."

"If you could be less dramatic, Cobb, it would be better," suggested Mr. Bangwell.

"Let him tell his story his own way," said Mrs. Bangwell.

Cobb promptly took advantage of the advocacy of his mistress and proceeded. Such an opportunity for the display of his elocutionary powers might never occur again.

"Ha! ha! ses I," he resumed, "what dark deed is now afloat, for the ways of that person was sneaky and snake-like. So, standing back in the shadder of the stairway, I watches him.

"Softly, stealthifully, he goes into the dormitory, up to Mister Wyburn's box, and, after a careful look round, he whips out a brown-paper parcel and tucks it away under the clothes. Then he comes out and goes downstairs like a flash of light."

"You saw his face?" said Mr. Bangwell, who was pale with excitement.

"Me did, sir," replied Cobb; "once, twice, thrice."

"It was not Wyburn?"

"No, sir, it was *not*. Nuthin' like him."

"Cobb," said Mr. Bangwell, in an agitated voice, "why did you not tell me of this earlier in the day?"

"In the fust place," said Cobb, "I thought it was only some lark, such as boys is given to, and I was nearly convinced of it when I went into the dormitory and just felt of the parcel. It seemed to be full of nails, but I couldn't look into it, for the breakfast-bell rang and I had to come down to wait at table.

"And, in the second place," added Cobb, in tones of softened reproach, "I didn't know nuthin' about the robbery, for it seems to me that when anything goes wrong I'm about the last pusson in the house who's asked to put it right, although, mind you, I'm more behind the scenes than you think. Biffins' nowhere."

"But who was it who put the parcel in the box?" asked Mr. Bangwell.

"*Ned Goran!*" cried Cobb, throwing up his arms; "Goran, who, in my heyes, have been a unmitigaitered willin."

"Are you prepared to repeat this to his face?" said Mr. Bangwell.

"Confront me with him and see," said Cobb.

CHAPTER XXXIV.
IN THE HOUR OF TRIUMPH.

ED GORAN and Ben Chicks had obtained leave to spend an hour in the town.

They elected to pass it in the seclusion of the parlour of a small public-house in one of the bye-streets.

It was not their usual habit to frequent such places, but they wanted to be by themselves, so as to fully enjoy their hour of triumph.

A jug of beer and two glasses were on the table. Each had a cigarette in his mouth.

"It was neatly done," said Ned Goran, sending a long, thin line of smoke from between his lips.

"Yes," returned Ben Chicks, "but I don't half like it. Suppose you had been found out."

"Impossible," said Goran; "it was too cleverly executed."

"Well, he goes to-night," said Chicks, "and there will be an end of him."

"The train leaves at 7.45," said Goran. "Of course you will go and see him off?"

"Yes, it will be a bit of a lark," replied Chicks; "we shall be able to make matters even with half-a-dozen words. But perhaps he will show fight."

"If he does we will lock him up," said Goran. "There is no need for any consideration to a thief."

"Goran," said Chicks, "I think you have a lot of the devil in you!"

"Some," answered Goran; "but what's the time? A quarter past seven. Drink up—we must be off. It will take us twenty minutes to get to the station."

Now Moatborough Station was well out of the town, and in the most inconvenient spot that could have been selected for it.

But that did not matter, as very little business was done there.

With a sense of triumph that was very pleasing upon them, the two conspirators wended their way to the station, and there they waited in vain for Jack's coming.

The train came in and started again without his appearing.

"Hang it!" said Chicks. "What does this mean?"

"Surely Bangwell can't have turned soft," muttered Goran. "He said he should go."

With a considerable change in their triumphant temperature the precious pair walked back to school, arriving there a few minutes after eight o'clock.

They were met at the door by Biffins, who said that Mr. Bangwell wanted to see them "particularly."

Getting lower and lower in feeling, and with a vague sense of a coming catastrophe, they ascended the stairs, and were admitted into the sitting-room.

Mr. and Mrs. Bangwell and both the ushers were there, all looking very grave.

No greeting was given them. Mr. Bangwell simply rang the bell twice.

This was a pre-arranged signal for Cobb to appear.

"Cobb," said Mr. Bangwell, "repeat your story."

This Cobb did, not varying an incident and scarcely a word. Dumb with dismay stood Ned Goran and Ben Chicks.

So totally unprepared for a revelation of this nature were they, that on being asked if they desired to question Cobb, they could only stare, wild-eyed, at that saviour of innocent youth.

"Dare you deny it?" thundered Mr. Bangwell.

"It was Chicks who wanted it done," gasped Ned.

"You liar!" replied Chicks. "It was you who arranged the whole thing. I was always against it."

"Silence, both of you, now that you have admitted your guilt," said Mr. Bangwell. "And I may tell you both that I have had some faint—it was very faint—suspicion of you, owing to the fact that the things you said were lost were not in the parcel. It appears to me that you never had them to lose."

They did not answer, and by their silence admitted the correct nature of the inference.

"And now I think of it," said Mr. Bangwell, "Wyburn must have missed them too. He suspected you also. Nay, I fancy he was sure of it. Cobb, you may go."

Cobb bowed, and, with a smiling face, departed.

Mr. Bangwell turned again to the crestfallen conspirators, and first addressed Ned Goran.

"On you," he said, "a heavy punishment must fall. Here, for some time, you have had a home, and I have treated you as a son. Now you forfeit all that. You might in time, as I intended, have succeeded me as master of this school. That is now impossible. You will have to go into the world and shift for yourself. You are old enough to do so."

"Who am I—what am I?" asked Ned Goran.

"The son of a friend of mine," replied Mr. Bangwell, sternly, "who imposed upon me in many ways, and died deep in debt with all who would trust him."

Ned Goran hung his head. His humiliation was complete.

"I shall send you to London," said Mr. Bangwell, after a pause, "and there you must get some form of employment. I will pay your lodgings for three months, and nothing more. After that I have done with you."

To Chicks he simply said—

"You will pack your box and be prepared to leave early to-morrow morning. To-night you will sleep in the spare room. I think it advisable for you to hold no further communication with the boys. Mr. Philpot, see that he does as he is told."

Mr. Bangwell turned his back upon the two disgraced boys, and the usher, rising, beckoned them from the room.

CHAPTER XXXV.

THE LAST OF CHICKS AND GORAN — BIFFINS ENTERS ON TROUBLED TIMES AND COMES TO A FULL STOP.

LARING at each other like bitter foes, Goran and Chicks followed Mr. Philpot, and, as soon as they were outside, began to recriminate each other.

"It was you who planned it!" said Ben Chicks.

"It wasn't! You arranged it all," replied Ned Goran.

And so they went on half-way down the corridor; then they lost all control of themselves, and fell upon each other tooth and nail.

"Bless me! What's this?" exclaimed Mr. Philpot, turning round.

Locked in close embrace, they had fallen to the ground, and were literally tearing each other like young savages.

In vain Mr. Philpot implored them to desist, and endeavoured to drag them apart.

Regardless of his efforts and entreaties they fought, cursing each other in a most horrible way.

The noise they made speedily drew a number of the boys upon the scene, which they surveyed with amazement.

At last Mr. Bangwell appeared, cane in hand, and he speedily put an end to it.

Three or four smart cuts chilled their fighting ardour, and, letting go of each other, they scrambled to their feet.

"You haven't any right to hit me now," said Ned Goran, fiercely.

"Get out of my sight!" was the answer of the schoolmaster; "and, understand this, if you make any further disturbance I will send for the police. In that case I may be induced to enter a charge of conspiracy against you."

This threat cowed them, and they slunk away, followed by a hiss or two from the boys, some of whom had already learnt the whole story.

"Don't make that noise, boys," said Harry Farnborough. "They are not worth it. Come down. Jack will soon be in the class-room."

. . . . . .

When Jack appeared there about half an hour later, he received a greeting that did much towards making amends for recent suffering.

We need not go into the details of it, but the cheering was heard in the kitchen—indeed, all over the house—and nobody was sent in to ask what was the matter.

After the first outburst was over Cecil Mead proposed that Cobb should be fetched in, and Bob Rudge went in search of him.

He found him in the hall, walking slowly to and fro, with his arms folded, like some knight of old, pacing a baronial chamber.

"Come on!" cried Bob. "They want you."

"Indeed!" replied Cobb, in deep tones. "'Tis well. I am prepared, but I do not seek high honours. Your thanks will suffice."

Nor would he receive anything for himself, although it was urged that a subscription ought to be set on foot for a testimonial.

"Gentlemen," he said, from the summit of Mr. Philpot's stool, whereon they had hoisted him, "the glory of this hour would be ruined by a gift to me; but there is one I love. If you can think of anything suitable for 'Melia, she will be glad of it. May I suggest that it be something in the way of attire. She wants it, poor girl!"

And then he told them that 'Melia was under his mother's protection in his "humble cottage home," and there she would remain until she got a place suited to "her talents."

At Cobb's instigation the tide of generosity turned towards Amelia, and a subscription was opened for her.

Those who had money gave liberally, and those who had not put their names down for something, promising to pay when "they got a remittance from home."

The next morning, while the boys were in the class-room, Ben Chicks and Ned Goran left the house, almost at the same hour.

From that time their ways of life divided, one going up and the other down the line, so that there seemed little prospect of their ever meeting again.

Whether they did so or not has nothing to do with our present story. Let it suffice to state that they left with a deep hatred for each other, deeper even than that they had felt towards Jack Wyburn.

When knaves fall out their hatred is indeed intense.

Leaving them, we must keep our attention fixed upon the other characters in our little drama of school life.

Somehow the story of Jack's wrongs and the restitution of his good name was immediately made known in the establishment of Miss Fillwell, and no less than eleven of the girls privately wrote a line of congratulation to Jack, and surreptitiously posted the same the next day when out " on parade."

Jack got their letters, and was very pleased to find he was such an object of interest to the " dear girls," but one letter, above all, delighted him.

That, of course, came from Fanny Whymper.

It was full of girlish sympathy, and some vital force was spent in bestowing her compliments on the departed conspirators, finishing up with the declaration that she would " like to scratch them."

And the probability was that, with a fair opportunity, she would have performed that feminine operation upon the precious pair.

While we are dwelling on the fair sex we may state that the testimonial to 'Melia took the form of a " thunder-and-lightning " shot silk dress, cheapened by being somewhat out of fashion, but none the less appreciated by the receiver.

Cobb was entrusted with delivering it, with " the compliments of the boys of Bangwell School, in recognition of the meritorious conduct of Cobb, her devoted admirer."

Cobb got leave the next Sunday to go home and present the testimonial, and on his return he assured the boys that " 'Melia wept with gratitude."

Of all the establishment only one did not approve of the turn affairs had taken, and that was Biffins.

It was not so much that he bore any affection for Chicks and Goran as his innate dislike to boys in general.

He was not usually demonstrative, but it was generally true that when a boy was in trouble Biffins, in a reserved way, was very happy.

Unfortunately for his peace of mind he, on this occasion, laid aside his reserve, and openly declared that the whole business was " bosh."

" He didn't happen to take them particular things," he said ; " but he's no better than those which have been sent away."

This utterance, thoughtlessly given vent to in the presence of Cobb, was duly reported to the boys, and a flood of indignation set in which threatened to wash Biffins clean out of the place.

For several days he did not know a moment's peace.

If he entered a room which could be fastened on the outside by lock or bar, so surely would he be imprisoned.

As he walked about the passages he was pelted from the staircase or the floors above with missiles which, if not very destructive, were objectionable.

At all times and all seasons he was subject to reproaches and cutting forms of chaff, which were very exasperating to his highly sensitive nature.

Eventually his tormentors ventured to invade even his private domain—the kitchen.

Perhaps he would be sitting in a comfortable position before the fire, chatting with the cook, when a bold young marauder would appear and make some remark which he considered offensive, such as—

" Is that fellow here still ? How can you put up with him, cookey?" or, "Mr. Bangwell's compliments, and he wants to know if you are glued to that chair. Get up and go to work, or you'll get the sack."

At last the aggressiveness of the boys took the form of—peas.

Bob Rudge started it.

Wandering about the town one morning he saw some pea-shooters for sale, and, happening by chance to have a copper in his pocket, he bought one, with an allowance of peas.

On his way back to school it flashed upon him that the shooter was the very thing for Biffins.

The idea took root.

Other boys said it was the thing, and there was a run upon pea-shooters.

Then Biffins entered into torment.

From out of dark corners and secret places, from above when he was below, and from below when he was above, the forcible and stinging pea found him out.

Wherever he went he found a pea to tread upon, or a pea found him.

His only time of rest was when the boys were in the class-room.

He talked of complaining to Mr. Bangwell, but lacking evidence as to the identity of any special enemy, he was obliged to give up the idea and sweep up the peas.

At last the climax came.

He was seated alone in the kitchen one evening, it being the day out for the cook and Cobb, and the other servants were upstairs, when the enemy in force descended upon him.

Biffins was meditating on the pros and cons.—the possible profit and loss—of marrying the cook, and taking a small public-house, when a perfect shower of peas was poured upon him.

Springing up, he saw half-a-dozen boys, just inside the kitchen, firing away like young Gatling guns.

" You little beasts !" he yelled ; " I'll murder you."

Seizing the kitchen poker, he sprang to his feet, and looked so horribly in earnest that the young warriors fled.

Biffins had lost all control of himself, and dashed madly in pursuit.

The flying foe made for the schoolroom, where their chums were assembled ; but, finding that Biffins, with his long legs, was gaining ground, they turned aside into the receiving room for visitors, a small apartment on the ground-floor.

Bob Rudge and Harry Farnborough, the leaders of the party, tried to close the door and fasten it, but Biffins had got his head and shoulders in.

" Help ! push here," cried Harry, and the rest in a body threw themselves against the door.

The result exceeded their expectations.

Not only was Biffins prevented from forcing his way into the room, but they completely disabled him.

His face was seen to lose all colour, his mouth opened, his eyes started, and he dropped the poker.

" Easy, boys !" cried Harry ; " we've hurt him."

They opened the door, and Biffins fell half in and half out the room.

There was a brief rolling of his eyes, a convulsive movement of the limbs, and he was still.

" We've killed him !" gasped Bob Rudge.

" See if he's breathing !" cried Tom Drake, who was of the party.

Harry Farnborough bent his head down and listened, but he could not hear his breathing

"We've done it," he said; "he's dead enough. But"—here he looked around—"who is to know *if we don't tell?*"

"Come away," said Bob Rudge, with a sickly smile; "let's go away somewhere and swear ourselves to secrecy."

"Hurry up," said Harry Farnborough. "I hear somebody coming."

It was not exactly to their taste, but in going out they had to step over the body of Biffins, which they did with a shudder.

Harry Farnborough went out last.

"Go on, boys," he said; "I'll soon follow."

CHAPTER XXXVI.

BOB RUDGE GETS A TURN, WHICH HE RETURNS WITH INTEREST.

 S Bob closed the door of the dormitory he said—

"It will never do to trust anybody with the secret."

Into this place they had gone to take the oath of secrecy.

They were all there—very grave, but none so grave as Harry.

"I can see how we did it," he said; "we pressed upon his heart and stopped the action of it."

"I suppose we all pressed a little?" said Bob, with a groan.

"Of course," said Harry, "all are in it equally. No shirking by anybody. It is sure to be found out. I don't think it's safe to stop here—not all of us."

"Where are we to go to?" asked Tom Drake, looking steadily at Harry.

"*I* shall go to sea," replied Harry. "We are all right for a week."

"A week!"

"Yes—I stayed behind to put the body in the cupboard. It won't be found until *it's going wrong.*"

"Oh! don't," pleaded Bob.

"Well, I won't," said Harry. "Now, mind this, not a word below. All you fellows go down but Bob and me. I want to have a word with him alone."

The others departed with alacrity, and Harry, having given them time to clear away, turned to Bob, and said—

"You ought to be grateful to me for what I've done for you to-night."

"Oh! yes," said Bob, faintly; "but what *is* it you did?"

"Covered you."

"Covered me?"

"Yes. It was *you* who really killed Biffin. You threw your whole weight against the door; the others only used up half of theirs."

"How do you know that?" demanded Bob.

"Come, now," said Harry, "didn't you do *all* you could to squash him?"

"Yes, I did," replied Bob, candidly.

"Just so; and nobody else did—and there you are. If it comes to a public trial the whole thing must come out, and it will fall upon you."

Bob Rudge stared aghast.

He could not deny that he had done his best to give Biffins a nip he would remember for awhile; but, of course, he had no intention of killing him.

However, he was dead, and somebody would have to suffer for it.

"Keep cool," said Harry, "and make your preparations steadily. Pack up what you think you will want. The best way of getting down to the sea is in a coal-barge—those fellows will give you a lift for a trifle. I'll just go and see how the wind lies. Keep your pecker up."

Harry, with a friendly and encouraging nod, left Bob, who, in a state bordering on despair, went to his box and began to pick out a few necessaries.

"Oh! what will mother say?" he ejaculated, with a sob. "It will break her heart, and father's too. He would warm me. What a beastly old fool Biffins must be to die like that!"

He had got a little pile of things on the floor ready to make into a parcel, when he heard a slight movement by the door.

Looking in that direction, he beheld something that turned his whole body to ice.

It was Biffins, standing just within the room gazing at Bob with a look of intense hatred.

"You sent for me, Mister Rudge," he said, in sepulchral tones.

"No-o-o!" stammered Bob.

"But Mister Farnborough said you did," replied Biffins. "He told me you would give me sixpence if I helped you to pack, and so I came."

With a wild cry of delight Bob sprang to his feet.

"You ain't dead, then?" he cried.

"No," replied Biffins, surlily; "but I shammed a bit to frighten some of you, and I'd a shammed longer, but Mister Farnborough stopped behind when you went away, and, taking a pin out of his jacket, stuck it here," he indicated the spot, "and up I jumps and he ran off. I don't bear no malice, but this sort o' thing have got to be put a stop to, or there'll be serious work."

"Biffins," said Bob, drawing a deep breath, "I don't want you to pack. It's all a mistake, but if you like you can earn sixpence. I'll give it to you the next time I get some pocket-money.'

"Honour?" said Biffins.

"Honour," repeated Bob.

"Then tell me what I've got to do, and I'll do it," said Biffins.

"Go back to Harry Farnborough," said Bob, "and tell him the moment you entered the room I fell on my back and haven't moved or breathed since."

"But will he believe me?"

"You go and try him. Just tell it to him as if you believed it was all over with me."

"I'll do it," said Biffins, with a malicious grin. "I owe Mister Farnborough a turn for that pin business."

For once in his life Biffins entered into a joke, and Bob, for the first and last time, leagued himself with Biffins.

Left to himself, Bob dropped quietly to the floor, and composed himself so that he looked as if he had given up the ghost.

In a minute or so he heard a quick step on the stairs, and Harry Farnborough burst into the room.

Bob held his breath as his chum threw himself down beside him.

"Oh! Bob—Bob, old man," he said, "what have I done to you?"

"Nothing," replied Bob, as he opened his eyes. "Nothing," he repeated, as he sat up. "Nothing," he said, for a third time, as he deliberately got upon his feet. "You tried to scare me and failed, so it was my turn to give you a turn, and I've done it."

"You have," replied Harry, with a long-drawn breath; "there's no denying it. You've got the best of this joke, and I ought not to begrudge you a little success just for a change. I say, Bob, you won't speak about this, will you?"

"Why not?" asked Bob. "You have had many a go in at me."

"What price for silence?" asked Harry, who, it must be confessed, like other jokers, had a great objection to being laughed at.

"Two shillings," replied Bob.

"Too much."

"I won't take less than eighteenpence."

"Well, eighteenpence be it. I'll give you an I.O.U. for it."

And having thus amicably arranged matters they adjourned below.

There, of course, they found Tom Drake and the others, who right through had thoroughly understood that the idea of Biffins being dead was a joke.

Bob frowned at them as they laughed, but said nothing, and so ended the matter.

CHAPTER XXXVII.

THE FORGED LETTER—THE MYSTERIOUS BELL AGAIN.

ESTORED to his old position in the school, Jack had leisure to think of general matters, and his mind soon called back the fact that he had in his possession some important letters.

They were given to him as epistles sent by Fanny Whymper to Ned Goran, and Jack had received them from Cecil Mead.

If written by the girl, she was no longer worthy of a single thought from Jack, for they were fulsome, flippant, and silly.

Jack read them with a feeling akin to disgust, and refused utterly to believe that Fanny had written them.

A close comparison of them with the letters he had received himself led him to conclude they were forgeries.

He said as much to Cecil Mead, who simply said he hoped it was so—"it was no affair of his."

"But you made it your affair, you know," said Jack.

Cecil turned his eyes upon his friend, looking him full in the face.

"Jack," he said, "if you want me to believe it, I will. I showed them to you for your sake—not for mine. I admire Fanny Whymper very much, but I don't believe in her. Don't let her shadow come between us."

"We had better not speak of her again," said Jack.

He handed the letters back to Cecil, who put them into his pocket, and, strange to say, Cecil received that very day conclusive proofs of the real nature of the missives.

A lot of waste-paper was brought out of Ned Goran's room, and temporarily placed by Cobb in a heap just outside the door.

Being left there for a time, the wind scattered the paper about the place, and when the boys came out in the evening some of it had been whirled round to the front of the house.

Cecil picked up two or three pieces, and, glancing at them, saw that they were copies of the letters he had in his possession. The writing was something like Fanny Whymper's, but not exactly so.

Then the truth flashed upon him.

Here were the early efforts of forgery on the part of Ned Goran—the papers on which he had practised before he became perfect.

Always clever with his pen, he had not hesitated to turn his gift to base uses.

"What a scoundrel he was!" thought Cecil. "Jack was right. He always is. Heigho! I think I should like to go away from here."

But of course he did not go, and the days passed by without any exciting event, save that the mysterious ringer of the bell twice again aroused the house in the middle of the night.

It had been an aggravating thing from the first, but now it was quite serious.

The greater part of those in the house firmly believed that it was rung by no mortal hand.

On Biffins fell a deadly fear, and he begged to be allowed to sleep "where he wasn't quite so lonely."

His request was considered a reasonable one, and, to Cobb's great disgust, Biffins' bed was put into his room.

About this time Mike Feeley and Buck Gruesum were released from prison, and it was reported that they were living together.

During their incarceration, Mrs. Gruesum, acting on the advice of the vicar, had left the town, taking her son with her.

Whither she had gone was not generally known, but it was rumoured that the vicar had obtained a place for her where Gruesum was not likely to find her.

She took nothing with her but wearing apparel and on his release Gruesum sold the furniture.

He said little about his wife, but, as some of the neighbours said, "he looked a great deal," and they wouldn't like the vicar to meet him in a lonely place after dark.

Shortly after rumours of a boy frequenting the cottage where Mike Feeley lived got about, and it was whispered that he was one of the Bangwell Boys.

It was also declared that he had been seen there late at night, or, what was the same thing—his shadow on the blind.

CHAPTER XXXVIII.

AT THE TRYSTING-SPOT — VERY STRANGE — AN ABSENTEE FROM SCHOOL.

IN due time the rumours referred to in the last chapter reached Mr. Bangwell's ears, but he pooh-poohed them.

Nevertheless, he took the precaution to lock all doors himself and take the keys up to his room.

One evening—the nights were drawing in now—Jack went to a spot on the banks of the river where he had appointed to meet Fanny Whymper.

She had been favoured with one of those rare holidays to visit some relations, and purposed to make her stay short, so as to see him for a little while.

The riverside was chosen because Miss Fillwell rarely went there, and the chances of discovery were reduced to a minimum.

Jack was not troubled with any fears about his old foes, Gruesum and Feeley, and it was without any undue trembling that he drew near the cottage where they resided.

He was passing the gate when he heard the sound of voices raised in anger, and he easily distinguished three he knew—Gruesum's, Mike Feeley's, and Harold Gillispie's.

An irresistible impulse led him to stop, and the next moment Harold emerged from the cottage, his face flushed with anger.

"I will make you sorely repent of this—both of you," he was saying; "it's a robbery—shameful and shameless."

Then he caught sight of Jack, and addressed him with an increase of violence in his angry tone—

"You here—spying upon me? What do you mean by it?"

"I am not spying upon you," replied Jack; "it was by the merest accident that I happened to be passing at this moment—that is, an accident as far as you are concerned."

"Why don't you go for him, youngster?" sneered Buck Gruesum, appearing at the door; "you ought to be able to spoil his pretty face."

"Gillispie," said Jack, quietly, "don't listen to that blackguard. I tell you truly that I had no idea you were here. It's been my misfortune to find you in bad company more than once—"

"That's a lie!" interposed Gillispie, hotly.

"Well, if you like to say so, I won't dispute it now," said Jack, quietly; "but to-morrow I shall ask you to recall your denial."

"To-morrow," said Gillispie, with a strange smile. "To-morrow. Ah! then I may not be able to do so."

Turning to Gruesum, he went on—

"Bear in mind what I tell you, or it will be the worse for you."

Buck Gruesum snapped his fingers.

"Do your worst—you can prove nothing."

Jack walked on, and when he got a little distance away he looked back and saw the boy standing on a small mound near the cottage, still speaking to Gruesum.

The light of the evening sun was on his lithe, straight figure and handsome face. His air, although he was speaking hotly, was dignified, and every movement he made was graceful and effective.

Jack was sure that he had never seen such a handsome fellow before, and the fact of his being found in low company seemed more than ever painful.

"He looks like a picture," thought Jack—"almost a lovely picture with that light about him. What infatuation is it that draws him into the company of such men as Gruesum? Ah! he is going back again."

As he spoke Harold stepped down from the mound, out of sunlight into shadow, and it appeared to Jack as if a total change had taken place in his appearance.

The grace of action was gone, and in its place were the remnants of one who is by some invisible power dragged along a road against his will.

A moment later and he had disappeared.

"He is lost," said Jack. "I can't help him, poor fellow! It's drink and gambling, I suppose. But what company for one so naturally refined! What's that?"

He started back from a bunch of coarse, long grass growing a few feet from the river. For a moment, and a moment only, he thought he saw a form lying there.

It was that of Harold Gillispie, stretched upon his back, with his arms extended—a white, still face, turned skywards, and a deep gash upon his forehead.

"What was it?" asked Jack. "A fancy or a vision?"

Whatever it was it had gone, and the perspiration stood on Jack's brow—the outcome of sudden excitement.

He wiped it away and hurried on, late in keeping his appointment, for he found Fanny Whymper there before him.

Fanny was seated on the trunk of a fallen tree, which was lying parallel with the river. Upon her face was the shadow of reproach.

"I was just about going away," she said. "Why are you so late?"

"I will tell you," replied Jack, seating himself beside her.

He told her the story of Harold Gillispie, as far as he knew it, which interested her keenly.

"I have seen him," she said, "more than once, when I have been out walking with the girls. You say you like him?"

"Yes, I can't help it," replied Jack.

"I don't, nor any of the girls," said Fanny. "He seems to me to be a worthless fellow."

"I suppose I am a bit blind," said Jack, "for I really can't see it."

"And yet you know he is worthless."

"Well, appearances are against him."

"Jack," said Fanny, "you are blind. Blind as a bat. This Gillispie is bad, I tell you. We hate the very sight of him."

"That's all right, as far as I am concerned," said Jack; "of course I don't want you to be in love with him. How is Miss Fillwell?"

"Oh! don't ask me," said Fanny; "as bad as ever. But you are joking."

"Well, are all the other girls in health?"

"The other girls don't concern you, so don't ask about them. Oh! Jack, we are getting so tired of living with that old cat, you can't think."

"Indeed!"

"Yes, and we were talking of running away."

Jack saw a burly ruffian ducking a boy under the water.

"Where would you run away to, and with whom?" asked Jack.

"Ah! that's the question," said Fanny, reflectively. "The old days when knights succoured maidens in distress seem to be gone for ever."

"Don't you look on me as your knight?" said Jack, tenderly.

"Of course I do," replied Fanny; "but you haven't any armour, or sword, or feathers, or anything romantic."

So they talked on in the pleasant way of young lovers until the twilight deepened, and then Fanny said it was time for her to be going back to school.

"It is later than I thought," she said; "please forgive me if I hurry. You mustn't come any further than the bridge."

As they were walking along the towing-path they met Gruesum sauntering towards them.

He stared hard at them, and chuckled—

"You'd look queer, my pretty miss," he said, "if I blowed upon you to Miss Fillwell."

"Oh! what an awful man," whispered Fanny.

"Don't take any notice of him," said Jack. "It isn't likely Miss Fillwell would believe anything he says."

"I don't know," replied Fanny; "she's so ready to believe anything wrong about us."

When they got near the bridge they stopped for a moment in a quiet corner to say Good-night, and then Fanny hurried on.

Jack waited long enough to let her get about half the way home, and then he also sauntered back to the school.

It was quite dark when he arrived there. He had exceeded his time allowance, but there was nobody on the look-out to reprove him.

Of late he had been rather a privileged young fellow, and more than one rule of the school had been relaxed for his benefit.

Entering the schoolroom, he found the boys gathered round a fire—the first of the autumn season.

"Looks jolly—doesn't it?" said Bob Rudge.

"It's right enough," replied Jack, carelessly. "Has anybody seen Gillispie?"

"Do we ever see him?" asked Tom Drake.

"I ask," said Jack, "because I particularly want to know if he has returned."

"He came back about six o'clock," said a boy named Barker, "but he went out again."

"How soon after?"

"Almost directly."

"Which way did he go?"

"Down the High-street."

"Back to the riverside, of course," muttered Jack. "It's no business of mine where he is; but I just wanted to know," he said aloud.

"I say," said Bob, "Biffins is going to the bad."

"What do you mean by that?" asked Harry Farnborough. "Did he ever go to the good?"

"Oh! dry up," said Bob. "Cobb says there is something wrong with Biffins; he's pretty well sure he's committed murder."

"More romance," said Jack.

"I don't know about that," said Bob. "Biffins sleeps in Cobb's room, and Nutty says it's awful to hear him going on in his dreams; he has a nightmare every half-hour."

"Who?" asked Cecil Mead; "Cobb or Biffins?"

"Biffins," said Bob. "Cobb says something must be done, as he don't get a wink of sleep."

A great number of useful prescriptions were suggested for Biffins' benefit, but nobody could exactly say how he was to be induced to take them.

The subject was soon changed; in varied conversation the time passed, and in due course the boys went to bed.

As they were going upstairs Jack saw Mr. Bangwell and the ushers in anxious conference in the hall.

He fancied he heard the name of Gillispie, but was not quite sure.

Unable to ask a question, because it would be indiscreet to do so, he went to bed very uneasy about this strange lad, who, in an unaccountable way, scorned his advice and proffered friendship.

However, Jack was soon asleep, and heard nothing more about Gillispie until the morning—then he learnt that he was missing.

Mr. Bangwell, it was said, had been up all night seeking him, and was absent still.

Shortly after the boys were up, Mrs. Bangwell, on going to Gillispie's room, found a letter under the pin-cushion on the dressing-table.

It was not addressed to anyone in particular, but its contents were interesting to all—

"*Do not seek me or enquire after me, as I shall be gone to a place far away from here. I am tired of my life. Disgrace rests upon me. Please give my love to the boys, and tell them that I liked them better than they thought, but I was too unhappy to mix much with them. Good-bye, all.*"

There was but one inference which Jack could put upon this letter when he heard its contents, and that was—Harold Gillispie had committed suicide.

What should he do now?

Ought he to speak out, and tell all he knew?

But what good would that do?

"Let them think what they will," thought Jack; "I will not do or say anything to tarnish his name. Let the dead rest."

The inference he had formed was also drawn by others—although nobody knew anything of what Jack considered "the darker side of his history."

Mr. Bangwell came back about twelve o'clock after a fruitless search, and at once jumped to the same conclusion.

"He was a strange boy—with something he held in reserve," he said. "I see what it is now. His mind was affected."

"Who are his friends?" asked Mr. Philpot.

"He was sent here by a Mr. Barton, of Furnival's-inn," replied Mr. Bangwell. "I have wired to him, but at present have received no reply."

"Better wire again," suggested Mrs. Bangwell.

This was done, and in half an hour the two telegrams were returned.

Mr. Barton had gone away from Furnival's Inn, and left no address.

"This looks like a swindle," said Mr. Philpot.

"No," replied Mr. Bangwell, "I received a year's fee in advance. The money is all right. It is the poor boy who is all wrong. I shall have the river dragged without delay."

CHAPTER XXXIX.
FOUND.

ISFORTUNES or great disasters it is impossible to keep a secret, and in a very few hours Moatborough was fully acquainted with the story of Harold Gillispie's disappearance, and the theory deduced therefrom.

Volunteers to assist in finding him were not lacking, and half-a-dozen boats were soon afloat with men and boys with drags, and poles, and nets, to search the river for the missing boy.

In one boat half-a-dozen persons, consisting of the two tutors, Jack Wyburn, Harry Farnborough, Cecil Mead, Bob Rudge, and Tom Drake, were together, with some drags and a long pole with a hook at the end.

Jack stood at the bow of the boat with the "drags."

For the benefit of the reader who may have never seen such things, we mention that this well-known instrument for searching a river consists of a huge treble fish-hook of iron, attached to a rope.

It is cast ahead as far as it can go, and then slowly drawn back across the bottom of the river.

The boats divided, some going up and others down the river. Jack's boat was working within easy distance of Mike Feeley's cottage.

It was not accident that placed it there.

Jack, acting on an instinctive feeling, had chosen the spot, and the tutors acquiesced.

They were men, but they were poor hands in a case of emergency like this, and they yielded themselves as subordinates to the master spirit that was in Jack Wyburn.

Acting on his directions they took the oars, and Tom Drake steered.

Harry Farnborough used the pole and Bob Rudge filled a post he was eminently qualified for—that of looker on.

"Go easy," said Jack, as he cast the drag for the twentieth time. "Back water slowly. A little more to the right, Tom. Steady."

They were exactly opposite the cottage now, and Mike Feeley, accompanied by Buck Gruesum, came out and stood upon the bank.

Both were smoking, and put on an air of surprise which did not deceive Jack.

"What are you doing," cried Mike Feeley; "catching eels?"

No answer was given him, and Buck Gruesum laughed drily.

"Eels," he said; "not they. It's the bottom of the river they are trying to pull up. Pull away, young 'un. You'll have it presently."

"I may find something by-and-bye that will interest *you*," replied Jack.

"I don't care a hang what you find," growled Gruesum.

"We shall see," answered Jack.

The ruffian was evidently uneasy, for he bit his lip and glared at Jack, as Bob Rudge said, as if he would like to eat him.

The boat went on slowly down the river, Jack casting the drag this way and that, Harry Farnborough searching the bottom of the river with the pole. Gruesum and Feeley sauntered on, keeping up with them.

So they went on to a part of the river where there was a clump of rushes about twenty feet wide in the middle of the river.

It was called "The Island," and had once been firm enough to land upon, but the action of the stream had slowly washed the earth away and now only rushes were left.

As the boat drew up to this place Mike Feeley began to show signs of suppressed excitement.

His hands opened and shut nervously, and his eyes wandered fitfully to and fro. Buck Gruesum knitted his brows and compressed his lips.

Jack, standing well up in the bow of the boat could see over the clump of rushes, and, as he was about to cast the drag, he saw some dark object lying in the midst of it.

"Pull hard!" he cried. "Steer straight for the rushes."

"If you get aground there," cried Gruesum, "you won't get off again in a hurry."

"Pull!" cried Jack. "Do as I tell you."

The tutors bent to their oars, and half-a-dozen sturdy strokes drove the nose of the boat well into the rushes.

The dark object became clearer to Jack, and his heart beat tumultuously as he recognised a human body.

"Found!" he cried, in a voice that was heard far up and down the river. "Keep your seats, or you'll upset the boat."

Yes, there was a body, but as yet the face was hidden by the rushes.

Jack took the pole from Harry Farnborough's hands and parted them.

Then, in a moment, the memory of the vision he had seen the night before flashed upon him.

The form, the face, with a deep scar across the brow.

"Harold Gillispie!" he cried.

A cry of horror burst from all in the boat, but Jack became suddenly quiet.

CHAPTER XL.
THE MYSTERY OF THE BELL.

ENTLY inserting the hook into the clothes, Jack drew the body towards him. All eyes were fixed upon that face, and with one voice they cried—

"Harold Gillispie!"

Mike Feeley and Buck Gruesum did not remain. The latter said something to the former, and they hurriedly retreated towards their cottage.

Jack saw them going, and cried out—

"Stop, you two villains, and look upon your work."

Gruesum stopped, and turned upon him like a wild beast at bay.

"Our work!" he yelled. "What do you mean by that?"

Jack did not answer him. Whatever his suspicions might be, he had, as yet, no proof. He felt he had been somewhat hasty.

The tutors said as much, and Jack quietly agreed.

"The time has not yet come to speak out," he said. "Poor fellow! To meet with such an end as this. It shows what evil company may bring us to."

They were all trembling as they dragged the body into the boat, and reverently laid it in the fore-part of it.

That the boy was dead there was no earthly doubt. The terribly white face, the half-closed sightless eyes, the fallen jaw, all bore witness of the painful fact.

"We must get back to the landing-stage," said Jack, "and then send for the police."

In a state of feverish excitement the tutors bent to their oars and backed water.

Slowly, in spite of the warning of Buck Gruesum, the boat glided off the muddy bank, and when again in deep water was turned round.

"There is no chance of his being alive," said Jack, with a sob; "but be as quick as you can. A doctor ought to see him without delay."

As the boat glided back Mike Feeley disappeared into the cottage, but Buck Gruesum, breaking into a lumbering trot, followed it up.

"I'm a-coming to see who it is!" he bawled. "And I'd like to know how you fix it on me?"

No answer was given him. Jack did not even look at the brute, for all his attention was absorbed in contemplating the body of the boy.

"Yesterday so full of life," he said, softly, "and now—poor fellow—poor fellow! But he did not do it himself; they have murdered him."

The bridge appeared in sight, and close to it was the landing-stage.

Upon both some idlers were lounging about, and the moment they saw the boat the truth was guessed at.

"Found!" they cried.

Several tore away into the town with the news, telling everybody as they ran along. By the time the boat arrived at the landing-stage there was quite a little crowd of spectators upon the bridge.

A policeman cropped up, and in a minute a doctor was there also. The latter immediately declared life to be extinct.

"He has been dead some hours," he said.

"The body must be taken to the nearest inn," said the policeman. "I'll get a stretcher and bring somebody to help me."

"I wish he could be taken back to the school!" said Jack, wistfully; "it seems hard to have to leave him entirely among strangers."

"It must be done, for it is the law," said the doctor; "we cannot help ourselves. After the inquest he may be taken where his friends desire."

·   ·   ·   ·   ·   ·   ·

Gloom rested upon the schoolhouse that evening. There was no light laughter, no jesting among the boys. On everything and everybody in the house it seemed as if a blight had fallen.

And so it had—the blight of sadness. Even Biffins felt it, and he was heard to say that the school-bell ought to be tolled for the dead.

Cobb wept bitterly, and it came out that Harold Gillispie, in a quiet, unobtrusive way, had been very good to him.

"He was always kind and spoke nicely," he wailed, "and he's given me lots of sixpences."

"Which you never said a word about," said Biffins.

"Because he told me not to," replied Cobb. "He wasn't the sort to brag about every little thing he did."

It is only right that the dead should, as far as possible, be remembered only for the good they have done, and really nobody could speak ill of Harold Gillispie.

He had been odd in his ways, and was reserved beyond the ways of boyhood; but he had never done anything shabby or mean, nor injured anyone in any way whatever.

Jack alone had a distasteful task before him.

Now, indeed, he felt he must speak out—not to injure the name of Harold Gillispie, but to bring the murderers of the boy to justice.

It is true that everybody did not think it was a case of murder, but Jack was sure in his heart that Gruesum and Feeley could account for the manner of his death.

So Jack went to Mr. Bangwell and told all. It was a revelation to the schoolmaster, and fairly took his breath away.

"The last—the very last—I should have suspected," he said.

The next thing done was to communicate with the police, who counselled secrecy.

"We must watch these men a bit," they said, "and get into the cottage when they are both from home."

"But can you do that?" asked Mr. Bangwell.

"There are few locks we have not keys to fit," was the answer.

And thus matters were allowed to remain for that night at least, and at the usual hour the whole house retired to rest.

Cobb was in a state of ferment.

Such a lover of deep mystery could not well be otherwise.

He, like Jack Wyburn, was pretty sure that the boy had been murdered, and to trace his murderer or murderers would be a congenial task to 'Melia's admirer.

To sleep after he got to bed was impossible. He lay quite still, though, thinking over all sorts of plans for the solving of the mystery, putting himself in the place of the private detective, to whom was to be given all the glory of bringing the criminals to justice.

He had laid dreaming in this open-eyed way about an hour and a half when a movement in the direction of Biffins' bed aroused him from his meditations.

The room was not quite dark, for the blind was up, and the light of a lamp in the road shone through the window.

By means of it he saw Biffins getting stealthily out of bed.

That he was doing so in a secret way was apparent to Cobb. Scarcely making a sound, he dressed himself.

Then, with the candle-stick in his hand, he stole softly from the room.

Outside he struck a match, lighted the candle, and went softly downstairs.

"Hullo!" said Cobb to himself, "here's another mystery. What is his game?"

Cobb, with the private-detective instinct very strong upon him, determined to find out.

Slipping on his trousers, he hurried after Biffins, who had now reached the hall, where he was standing quite still, apparently listening.

Cobb looked over the banisters, and, espying him in this attitude, chuckled softly—

"All right," he thought. "Go it, Biffins. Cobb of the Silent Feet is on thy trail."

Biffins went on softly—stealthily.

Cobb followed, walking with naked feet, and not making a sound.

He reached the bottom of the stairs just in time to see Biffins open the door of the bell cupboard, and after a hurried glance round go inside.

"Ho—ho!" thought Cobb. "The mystery of the bell-ringing is about to be bust."

Cobb wasted no time in meditating upon his discovery; but glided upstairs with much swiftness of foot, and succeeded, by his knowledge of the place, in finding Mr. Bangwell's door in the dark.

There he knocked, and about at the same moment the bell gave out a single note.

"Blessed if he isn't going to toll it for a change!" muttered Cobb.

"Who's there?" asked Mr. Bangwell.

"Me, sir—Cobb!" replied that youth through the keyhole.

"What do you want?"

Ding! went the bell.

"Come down, sir," said Cobb. "I've found out who is ringing the bell."

Dong! went the bell.

It was a poor bell, as bells go; but the sound of it sounded very sad and solemn in the stillness of the night.

Mr. Bangwell was heard to be dressing himself hurriedly, and in a few moments the door was opened.

He held a lighted candle in his hand, and his face was very white.

Ding! went the bell.

"Who is it ringing?" he asked.

"Biffins, sir," replied Cobb; "you can catch him at it now easy."

Dong! went the bell.

"This is worse than all," said Mr. Bangwell—"a horrible mockery. Oh! here you are. Come down with me."

It was the two ushers, who had just turned out of the room below like a pair of scared rabbits.

"We have got the bell-ringer now," said Mr. Bangwell. "Come quietly, gentlemen. Cobb, lead the way."

Cobb was not averse to assuming the position of leader. Anything for glory.

So the four went downstairs without a sound.

And on the way the bell, at intervals, gave out its dolorous note.

"The daring scoundrel!" thought Mr. Bangwell. "I'll wring his neck for him!"

The door of the bell-chamber was open, and a candle was burning inside.

By its light Biffins was revealed, calmly and steadily pulling the rope.

"You villain!" said Mr. Bangwell, rushing in. "How dare you make that confounded noise?"

Biffins did not answer him or even look round.

He took no notice of his master at all.

Once more he pulled the rope, and Mr. Bangwell, in his anger, raised his hand to strike him.

But at the same moment Biffins turned his face to his master, and fixed upon him a pair of *sightless eyes*.

There was no meaning, no lustre of life in them. They might have been the eyes of a dead man.

"Merciful Heaven!" exclaimed Mr. Bangwell, "*the man's asleep*."

And so he was.

Biffins was a somnambulist when under the influence of great excitement.

Badgered and bullied in his earlier days at the school about the feeble way he had rung the bell, he had been in the habit of occasionally getting up in the night and giving it a bit of a ring.

The excitement of the recent day had also acted upon him, and there he was, tolling the bell for the poor boy who had been found in the river.

"Stand still," said Mr. Bangwell, breathlessly. "It would never do to awaken him. The shock might be fatal."

As it happened, Cobb had finished his ringing, and, letting go of the rope, he picked up his candlestick and went slowly back to his bedroom.

They watched him while he undressed again, blew out the candle, and got into bed.

Immediately he began to snore prodigiously, just in the way he had been heard to snore on previous occasions when the bell had aroused the house.

"He will be all right now," said Mr. Bangwell. "Are you afraid to sleep here to-night?"

"No, sir," replied Cobb. "I ain't fallen so low as to be afraid of Biffins, asleep or awake."

"Very good," said Mr. Bangwell, with a faint smile. "It will be for this night only. To-morrow I shall give him a month's wages and discharge him. A somnambulist in a school is not quite the thing."

And on the morrow Mr. Bangwell was as good as his word.

He told Biffins of his infirmity, explained that it was out of place in his academy, paid him his money, and gave him the sack.

. . . . .

The discovery of the somnambulistic tendencies of the departed Biffins was an immense relief to everybody in the house, for, with few exceptions, they had learnt to look upon the bell-ringing as a supernatural piece of work.

On that account Cobb was made much of, and again was a hero.

He bore his honours with commendable modesty, and accepted the presents that were bestowed upon.

Mr. Bangwell, knowing his musical tendencies, gave him a zither, on condition that he did not practise it on the tiles at night.

The perilous position he had been seen in there, and from which he was happily rescued without injury, was a thing to be avoided in the future.

Mrs. Bangwell raised his wages, and promoted him to the place of the departed Biffins. The tutors presented him with a penknife, and the boys gave him all sorts of odds and ends.

Likewise, the cook gave him something, but it was not so acceptable as the other things, being simply a box on the ear.

She did not like parting with her Biffins, and was especially inconsolable because his place would not be filled by another man.

Meanwhile, Mr. Bangwell had tried his best to

find the guardian of Harold Gillispie, as he assumed the writer of the letter was.

But nothing came of telegraphing, nor even of the hurried visit to London, so he put the matter into the hands of a private enquiry agent.

Then came the inquest, and the story of the poor boy—as far as it was known—was told, the body was sworn to, and the police asked for an adjournment.

They had suspicions of foul play, but declined to state in what direction their suspicions pointed.

Mike Feeley and Buck Gruesum both attended the inquest, but were not called as witnesses, which certainly seemed to be a relief to them.

The inquest was adjourned for a further medical examination and public enquiry.

Jack, of course, had been a witness, but, acting under the instructions of the police, said as little as possible.

Indeed, he said nothing to implicate a living creature.

There was no school that day, as might have been expected, and after the preliminary enquiry Jack went off for a walk by himself.

He frankly told two of his chums who offered to accompany him that he wished to be alone, although he could not have given a reason for the desire.

He sauntered off with no real purpose in his mind, thinking over recent events and trying to reconcile the various things which had recently come under his notice.

But he could not quite succeed. Harold Gillispie at school was strange, but his conduct there was not at all in harmony with a companionship with such ruffians as Gruesum and Feeley.

Jack could not piece matters together anyhow, and when he gave up the task with a sigh, he found himself close to the railway-station.

The signal had fallen for the afternoon down train, and he walked upon the platform to see who had come by it

This is a favourite amusement with people who live in the country and have time to indulge in it.

"She's a bit late to-day, sir," said the porter. "They've wired that there is a fog in London, and that always upsets us. I shouldn't like to live up there to be choked half my time."

"Oh! it's not quite so bad as that," replied Jack. "Here she is."

The train was coming round the corner, and the steam was shut off the engine.

In all the majesty of force and speed it glided to the platform, the brake was applied, and the train came to a standstill.

Jack was leaning carelessly against the ticket-office, with his hands in his pockets. He ran his eye up the train, and saw two doors open.

From one compartment descended an unmistakable commercial traveller, loud-voiced, cigar in mouth, making himself seen and heard.

Then from another compartment a slim, well-dressed youth descended, and all the life-blood in Jack's veins seemed to suddenly cease to flow.

It was Harold Gillispie, or his *ghost!*

———

CHAPTER XLI.

THE GHOST AND JACK—A VERY STRANGE STORY.

HICHEVER it was, Jack was not in a position to ask a question; but stood against the railings that fringed the station-yard, unable to do anything but stare.

There was no more movement in him than there would have been in a figure of stone. Meanwhile, the form of Harold Gillispie advanced towards him, stopping half-way to exchange a few words with a railway porter.

The man was not staggered or alarmed, but replied to him in the usual matter-of-fact way.

"That's no ghost!" thought Jack.

But still he did not stir.

On came the form, in the old leisurely, half-dreamy way, until within a few feet of Jack.

Then Harold Gillispie stopped short.

"How do you do, Wyburn? I am very glad to see you here."

The tone was a perfectly natural one, although the air was somewhat constrained.

"Is it you, Gillispie?" asked Jack.

"Of course. Who should it be?" was the rejoinder.

"I must have been dreaming," said Jack, passing a hand across his brow. "Only yesterday I saw you dead, and—"

A sad smile and a hand quickly raised checked him.

"Not me," was the answer; "but my twin-brother."

A tremendous flood of light poured suddenly in upon Jack It was too strong for him to see things clearly as yet. It was blinding, bewildering!

"Gillispie!" he gasped. "How was it you never told us?"

"Wyburn," said Gillispie, for it was indeed the boy in the flesh, "I could not say anything for *his* sake. Is there any place handy where you and I can have a quiet chat?"

"Come into the waiting-room," said Jack, drawing a deep breath; "there is sure to be nobody there just now."

The waiting-room was, as he expected, when they reached it quite deserted.

Jack closed the door.

"Gillispie," he said, "have you heard anything?"

"I have heard something terrible, which has brought me here. Oh! Jack—friend as I have longed to call you—it is a horrible story."

"Have you heard how he died?" asked Jack.

"Yes, and I think he has been murdered," replied Harold Gillispie.

"That is my opinion; and the murderers—who are they, do you think?"

"That man Gruesum and the old ruffian Feeley."

"So far all is in harmony with my thoughts," said Jack; "but let us begin at the beginning. Do your friends know of this?"

"Friends?" said Harold Gillispie. "I have no friends, in the relative sense. I have only a cold-blooded, matter-of-fact guardian—a wheezy old lawyer, who is abroad now."

"Did he live in Furnival's-inn?"

"Yes."

"Where is he now?"

"Somewhere abroad—at Mentone, I think. He is always ailing or fancying ills, and is perpetually shifting his place of abode. I heard from him two months ago, when he told me he was going away for a time."

"The clouds of mystery are clearing a bit," said Jack. "The poor fellow who is dead is your brother, you say."

"My brother Stephen," said Harold. "We were twins in birth; but, strange to say, not in feeling or sentiment. For several years he has been my *bête noir*—idle, dissipated, selfish, cruel. Understand me, I do not wish to condemn him. I only speak of these things to explain matters."

"I understand," said Jack; "but would you not like to reserve it until by-and-bye?"

"No," replied Harold. "I want to tell *you* all, because I have always felt for you the keenest friendship, but did not like to show it from a feeling of shame."

"Shame! What had you done?"

"Nothing; but it was one of the penalties of my twin life that while my poor brother went the evil way *I* had to bear the penalty. HE did not care, but *I* did. He disgraced himself, poor boy, wherever he went. To each of us was granted an allowance, very liberal indeed for our years, but he spent his and *mine*. He had a miserable infatuation for low company, drinking, and gambling. I am told that he inherited these things from one of our grandfathers; but I do not understand these matters —I leave all that to others to judge."

Harold stopped for a moment, put his hand upon his heart, as if he felt a pain there, and resumed—

"I need not recapitulate the long story of his errors; but let me tell you that he has been dismissed from school after school, and was virtually an outcast from all decent society. He laughed at decency—despised it, and was so far insensible to what is right and wrong between brothers as to follow me wherever I went, and prey upon my feeling of shame.

"When I came here," said Harold, lowering his voice, "I came in secret. But he soon found me out, and then began the old miserable life over again. The only thing he consented to was not to make his presence publicly known. That indeed suited him, for he had a liking for secret ways and the dark hours of night. Can you not guess the rest?"

———

CHAPTER XLII.

FAREWELL.

"I UNDERSTAND enough," said Jack, softly, "to see how all the mistakes we have made concerning you originated. I always liked you, Harold, in spite of many things that appeared so black against you. I could not make them fit in with you at all."

"My brother has paid the penalty of his folly, poor fellow," said Gillispie, after a pause. "I grieve for him—I must; but I fear that in no case would he have reformed."

"Come," said Jack, "it is time we went and explained matters to Mr. Bangwell and the rest. After that we must see what is to be done to bring the perpetrators of the crime, for crime I am sure it is, to justice."

"It will be some satisfaction to me," said Harold, with a mournful smile, "to be sure that Stephen did not commit suicide."

"He did *not*," replied Jack, with emphasis. "Of that be assured."

They left the waiting-room, and choosing the quiet ways, soon reached the school.

"I think I had better leave you in the hall for a few moments," said Jack, "just to explain the state of things to Bangwell."

As he spoke Cobb and Bob Rudge appeared, the former from the direction of the kitchen, the latter descending the stairs.

They stared first at Jack, then at Harold, and burst into a simultaneous howl.

"It's all right," cried Jack, hastily. "Harold's alive—twin brother—all a mistake."

It was just as well that he did explain things or the consequences might have been serious.

As soon as Sam got at the facts he bounded off to spread the news, and five minutes later everybody in the house had got the gist of the story.

That night Mike Feeley and Buck Gruesum were in the town drinking together.

This was a rare thing with them now, and, of course, did not pass without comment.

Their room in general was preferred to their company, but landlords, like beggars, cannnot be choosers, if their patrons behave themselves.

Any man has a right to be served in any inn if he can pay for what he wants and behaves himself.

Acting on this phase of the law, the two cronies went into some of the best houses and ordered drink.

In most places they were at first refused, but afterwards were supplied.

At last they presented themselves at the White Hart, the best inn in the town.

They expected to be refused peremptorily, but drink had made them contumacious if it had not intoxicated them, and they intended to insist upon their rights.

But to their surprise, the landlord on seeing them became at once amiable and obliging.

"Walk into the parlour, gentlemen," he said "You'll find a bit of fire, and there isn't too much company to trouble you."

Company, indeed, there was none, which, in their eyes, accounted for the landlord's politeness ; but they were wrong.

"*I'll bring you what you require* in a moment," he said, as he left the room.

It was, however, nearly five minutes before what they required appeared.

Buck Gruesum was about to ring the bell, when the door opened and four policemen appeared.

With astonishing celerity they handcuffed the staggered ruffians and bid them "come along quietly."

"What's it all for ?" asked Gruesum.

"You are charged with the murder of Stephen Gillispie," was the answer.

"It wasn't me," said Gruesum, caving in. "Feeley struck the blow."

"You liar !" cried the old sexton ; "you did it."

Losing, as it seemed, all thought of others being present, they proceeded to bandy accusations with each other, the officers mentally noting all that was said.   When the lull came one constable called their attention to the fact that all they said would be used against them.

"Yes," said old Mike Feeley, bitterly ; "and more fools we to blab.   But you always were a cur, Buck Gruesum."

"And you are a cold-blooded old villain," replied Gruesum.

And so they went on weaving for themselves and each other the rope that was to be put around their necks.

Great were the rejoicings in Moatborough when their arrest was known, and the news spread so rapidly that a considerable crowd gathered to escort them to the station.

The said crowd also displayed a burning desire to lynch them, and would have done it but for the police.

That night *both* made a full confession of the crime, which shut out all mercy for either.

In Feeley's cottage evidence of their complicity had also been found—signs of a deadly struggle, blood-stains on the wall, and a letter from poor misguided Stephen, reproaching them with having cheated him at cards, and expressing his resolve to call and have it "out with them."

The boy must have had some pluck ; but "having it out" proved fatal to him, and led to the series of exciting events we have recorded.

The details of the trial of the murderers would be out of place here.

Their crime was brought home to them, and they paid the penalty inside the county gaol, both going to the scaffold like curs, howling for their lives to be spared.

Merciless themselves, what right had they to hope for mercy ?

And now a time of peace settled upon Bangwell School, and our task is almost done.

It only remains for us to put on record that Harold remained there and gave up his isolated way of living—becoming, in short, one of the boys.

Between him and Jack a fast friendship was formed, without lessening any of the links of good fellowship already formed.

There were, as there had been before, agreeable flirtations with the girls, in spite of the dragon-like guardianship of Miss Fillwell, Jack and Fanny Whymper being especially serious in their devotion to each other, insomuch that it was considered they would in due time and season make a match of it.

There was, indeed, such a strong probability in it that we may look upon it as a settled thing.

Cobb remained true to 'Melia, and she to him, even when the exigencies of service temporarily divided them.

Time rolled on, and the boys went away one by one, as they do in all schools—Bob Rudge, Cecil Mead, Tom Drake, Harry Farnborough, and Jack and his friend Harold.

Others came to fill their places, but the exciting days of old never returned, and are now but legends in the school.

Jack is an officer in the P. and O. Company; Harold is a captain of Hussars, and the others we have heard of fill very good posts in the busy world.

Jack writes regularly to Fanny Whymper, and when " he gets his ship "—that is, becomes captain, he will marry.

Cobb has whiskers, and is butler to the Mayor of Moatborough.   He talks of marriage also.

Mr. Bangwell is very grey, and other tutors fill the places of Skaffer and Philpot.   Time changes all things.   Nothing in this wide world stands still.

And now let us, in conclusion, wish good fortune and happiness, wherever they may be or whatever their lot, to the little band we have known as the "Bangwell Boys."

THE END.